THREADS OF GRACE

ALSO BY KELLY LONG

Arms of Love

THE PATCH OF HEAVEN NOVELS

Sarah's Garden

Lilly's Wedding Quilt

Threads of Grace

STORIES INCLUDED IN

An Amish Christmas

An Amish Love

An Amish Wedding

An Amish Kitchen

THREADS OF GRACE

A Patch of Heaven Novel

Kelly Long

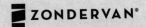

ZONDERVAN

Threads of Grace © 2013 by Kelly Long

This title is also available as an e-book.

Requests for information should be addressed to:
Zondervan, *3900 Sparks Dr. SE, Grand Rapids, Michigan 49546*

ISBN 978-0-7180-8176-8 (repack)
ISBN 978-0-310-35570-0 (mass market)
ISBN 978-1-4016-8813-4 (e-book)

Library of Congress Cataloging-in-Publication Data
Long, Kelly.
Threads of Grace: A Patch of Heaven Novel / Kelly Long.
pages cm.—(A Patch of Heaven Novel; 3)
ISBN 978–1–59554–872–6 (trade paper)
1. Amish—Fiction. 2. Love stories. 3. Christian fiction. I. Title.
PS3612.O497T48 2013
813'.6—dc23   2012040488

Printed in the United States of America

19 20 21 22 23 / QG / 6 5 4 3 2 1

For My Father

GLOSSARY OF PENNSYLVANIA DUTCH WORDS AND PHRASES

ach—an exclamation like *oh* or *my*

aentis—aunts

boppli—baby/infant

bruder—brother

daed—dad/father

danki—thank you

daudi haus—small house in back of the main house where the parents live after their children are grown and married

der Herr—God

eck—bridal table

Englisch—non-Amish people and their ways

es dutt mir leed—I am sorry

fater—father

fraa—wife

Gott—God

gut—good

hiya!—hi

hund—dog

jah—yes

kapp—prayer cap

kindskind—grandchild
kuche—cake
kinner—children
kumme—come
mamm—mother
munn—moon
narrisch—crazy
nee—no
redd-up—clean up
sei so gut—please
was en de welt—what in the world
wunderbaar—wonderful

PROLOGUE

Middle Hollow, Ohio

A late summer breeze caught the scent of the wild roses that spilled over the crumbling stone wall and filled Grace Raber's apron. Grace was eighteen, but because of her sunny disposition, those around her always thought of her as a much younger child. There was nothing she loved so much as the time after her chores, when she was at liberty to wander about the fields and trees near the family farm. She often brought things back to decorate the supper table under her *mamm's* approving eye.

Today God had given her roses, and their heady scent called up romantic images of a tall, blond-haired, blue-eyed Amish man, someone who would cherish her and love her forever.

The fantasy gave Grace the sense of floating, flying, defying gravity. But as she approached the farm, her steps grew heavy.

A horse and buggy stood out front, belonging to their neighbor, Silas Beiler. He was a stern old man who owned the adjoining property, and despite her parents' attempts to hide it, Grace knew that her family was in debt to him after a bad harvest the previous year.

Grace didn't like the Amish widower. She always felt as though the thickness of her dress and apron were never enough to shield her soul from the pious condemnation in the man's dark eyes. Whenever she passed by, he would raise his bushy eyebrows in an expression of pained contempt. Just the thought of him made her shudder.

But the roses were wilting in her apron, and she'd dallied long enough. She'd slip in through the back kitchen door, put them in water, and make herself scarce until he left. Thankfully, Mr. Beiler never accepted the courtesy of staying for a meal.

Holding her apron ends together with one hand, Grace eased open the screen door and slipped into the coolness of the kitchen.

Usually the chatter of her little brothers and sister filled the house, but today the kitchen was eerily silent.

Silent, but not empty.

Her *mamm* sat at the pine wood kitchen table with her head bent in her hands. Her father stood near her, his shoulders slumped and rounded while he aimlessly patted her mother's shoulder.

Only Silas Beiler stood erect, his hands clasped behind his back, his expression one of cold judgment. He looked up as Grace entered, and she felt the familiar chill that always descended upon her in his presence.

"*Mamm*, what's wrong?"

Her mother looked up as if surfacing from a fog. She grasped Grace's hand, and her sobs increased.

Grace looked to her father. *"Daed?"*

Her *fater* chewed at his bottom lip for a minute, then finally began to speak, not looking at Grace but at a spot beyond her on the wall. "Grace . . ."

His voice faltered, and Grace felt her heart begin to pound. "What is it?"

"Mr. Beiler here . . . well, we're deep in debt to him. I—I've borrowed a lot over the past year, and I can't seem to get it paid back."

"Tell the girl the truth," Mr. Beiler demanded. "You are a failure as a farmer and do not know how to save a penny, let alone a dime. You are in dire conditions through no fault but your own, and because the Lord will not reward the efforts of the wastrel. Your wife is sick with her lungs as punishment for your sins—"

"Stop it!" Grace cried. "How dare you speak to my father that way? What kind of man are you? What kind of Christian? Our people help one another without counting the cost—"

"Grace . . . *ach*, please don't." Her mother squeezed her hand.

Silas Beiler stared at Grace. His eyes glittered and a thin smile curved his lips. *"Nee,* let the girl go on. She's only showing the deficits I mentioned earlier. Which makes my proposal all the more gracious."

Grace turned to her father. "What proposal?"

Her father's blue eyes welled with tears. "Mr. Beiler has kindly offered to pay off all our debts, to him and to others. And provide money for the medicines for your mother's asthma. He will allow us to live and work on the farm as his tenants and will see that we have food and provisions and medicine if the year grows lean. We will not have to continually rely on the community. The bishop . . . the bishop approves of all of this."

"*Ach*," Grace murmured. How difficult it must be for her *fater* to submit to becoming the tenant of such a miserable man.

"There is only one thing that Mr. Beiler requests." Her father paused and drew a deep breath. "He asks for your hand in marriage."

Grace almost laughed. "What? You can't be serious?"

Then she saw the old man's spine stiffen. He *was* serious. Dead serious.

"But, *Fater*, I . . . he . . . surely not." She groped for words. "It is a . . . a kindness," she said, stumbling on the word. "Yes, a kind and generous offer, but truly not necessary."

Mr. Beiler drew himself up and scowled down his nose at her. "I assure you, girl, my offer is in full seriousness, and kindness has *nix* to do with it. The Lord has cursed you with a beauty that draws the eyes of man, but as my wife, you will learn discipline and compliance. I will, in fact, be saving your eternal soul. It is my duty, I have been convicted of this. I do not look forward to the burden, but I will be diligent. You may rest assured of that. Now, what is your answer—and I beg of you, girl, do not be a fool."

Grace struggled to breathe. For a moment or two she cast about wildly, a small animal caught in a trap. Her parents avoided her gaze. When at last her eye caught her father's, she saw a pleading in his expression, resignation mingled with grief. She was the eldest, called by the ways of her people to honor her father and mother, to help them. But she could not bring herself to say the words.

Instead she nodded once. Her father let out a sigh of relief. Her mother broke into a fresh round of sobbing.

"Very wise," Silas Beiler announced. "I will make all of the arrangements. Good day."

He walked across the scuffed pine floor and out the back door. In his wake, Grace looked down to see a single pink rose, trampled beneath his feet.

CHAPTER 1

Exactly how many women do you plan on kissing?"
Seth Wyse grinned at his older *bruder*, Jacob.
"As many as it takes."

The early morning sunlight of first summer played
through the open barn doors and highlighted the red-
dish tones in Jacob's long dark hair. Seth noticed with
curiosity the way that same light illuminated the
golden hairs on his own forearm. It amused him that
newcomers never took them for brothers. Although
both of them were tall and broad-shouldered, Seth had
blond hair, blue eyes, and a ready smile. Jacob had dark
hair, hazel eyes, and a brooding look about him.

"As many women as it takes to get the Widow Beiler
out of your head?" Jacob paused in currying the dark
mare and shot a frown in Seth's direction. "I thought
you were over her. Besides, you're starting to get more
of a reputation than you already have among the
women folk. One of these days some nice *mamm* is
going to catch you in action, harness you to a bride,
and that will be that."

Seth sighed and shifted on the bale of hay where he sat. He had been a bit over the top with the girls lately, but only because he was so frustrated trying to imagine what a kiss with Grace Beiler would be like. Still, Jacob was right about one thing: Seth was obsessed with the woman—had been since the first time he'd laid eyes on her.

"Seth!"

"What?" He snapped out of his reverie to meet Jacob's glare.

"For the third time, get up and do something. Get over her."

"It's not that easy. There's something in me that's drawn to the woman."

Jacob sighed. "*Ach*, it's the artist in you."

Maybe Jacob was right. Perhaps Seth's obsession with the lovely Widow Beiler did have some connection to his secret painting and charged dreams. But ever since Grace Beiler had moved to their small community a little over six months ago, he'd tried everything short of standing on his head to get her attention—or failing that, to get the desire to be near her out of his mind.

"At least Grace trusts you with her *sohn*," Jacob said.

"Yeah, because of you. And Lilly. She likes Lilly."

Jacob grinned. "I like Lilly too."

"That's right, big *bruder*. Go ahead and tease. You've got a wife you can't wait to go home to, a babe on the way, and you even have a dog. The perfect life."

Jacob rolled his eyes. "Do you want a *hund*?"

"I want her to pay attention to me," Seth said. "I just turned twenty-four. Maybe she thinks I'm too young. I wonder how old she is. Maybe if I was older, she'd look at me."

"Age has nothing to do with love."

"Danki," Seth said with a sour expression. "That helps a lot."

A small figure appeared in the doorway and both brothers looked up. It was young Abel Beiler, breathless and sobbing.

"What's wrong, Abel?" Seth moved toward the child. Abel had autism, a traumatic brain birth injury, and many developmental delays. He was hesitant with his trust. Seth had learned not to do anything with abrupt haste around the boy, as it only seemed to upset him.

The boy's violet eyes, so like his mother's, were huge in his pale face as he stared up at Seth. "Mama's hurt. Her legs are stuck. Under . . . under some rocks."

"Okay . . . okay. Tell me, slowly." Seth put a gentle hand on Abel's shaking shoulder. "Where is she?"

"In the garden at home. The rock wall fell down. She . . . she was planting flowers."

Seth glanced at Jacob. "I'll go."

Jacob stepped in front of him and held out his hand to the boy. "Abel, come here."

The child moved but still hiccupped with sobs. "I'm scared."

"I know," Jacob soothed. "I'll stay here with you, and Seth will go see to your *mamm*, all right? It's going to be okay."

Seth heard the words from a distance as he threw the reins over their fastest horse, and then he began to pray.

Grace winced as she tried to hoist herself up on her elbows. She'd been foolishly working near a low, unstable rock wall, attempting to do some repairs and plant some flowers. Her shoe had caught on a jagged stone and the whole thing had given way.

She blew a dark hair off her brow in exasperation. Her *kapp* was askew. Her right foot hurt badly, and she couldn't wriggle free of the weight of the stones. She had no choice but to send Abel to the Wyse farm for help.

She knew her son had been scared, and she uttered a prayer for his peace of mind. Yet she could not help hoping, as she gritted her teeth and tried another fruitless movement, that it would be Jacob Wyse who would come. Not Seth.

The less rational part of herself mocked her silent plea. *Of course you want Seth Wyse. Why else have you been avoiding him for six months?*

Grace groaned and caught a fierce grip on her wayward thoughts. True, she had been avoiding him, but only because he was so *obvious*. So sure of his charm. And so *young*.

She could avoid him, but she couldn't avoid the truth: for the first time in her life, she had met someone who attracted her. But for a hundred reasons, she couldn't take the chance. It was too soon. Everything was too raw. There was too much risk. Too much pain.

She had come to Pine Creek to get away, to heal. To protect herself and her *sohn*. She couldn't—wouldn't—jeopardize that for a handsome face and a quick smile.

Suddenly she heard the approaching hoofbeats of a single horse. Grace shielded her eyes against the summer sun and caught a glimpse of golden hair. She stifled a groan, anchored herself more sturdily on her elbows, and lifted her chin. She could strive for dignity, if nothing else.

He was off the horse and by her side in a moment. "Grace? How bad is it? Maybe we shouldn't move you."

He ran strong, practiced hands down the length of her legs to where the rocks lay. Shame burned like her skin at his touch, even through the fabric of her apron and dress.

"Do you mind?" she snapped.

He shot an incredulous look at her. "I'm trying to help you, not *touch* you."

"Es dutt mir leed," she apologized in a whisper. "Of course. I need help. It's mainly my right ankle, I think."

As he began to move the rocks away, she took a deep breath and concentrated on looking up at the blue sky. Waves of pain drifted through her. But more than the pain, she was aware of the clean, fresh scent of him, like linen and green grass and life itself.

She bit her lip as he reached the last bit of the wall.

"Can you move anything?" he asked.

She began to ease her left leg out from the debris. Her black shoe looked dented and mashed, but she flexed her ankle and bent her knee. "I think this leg's okay."

He exhaled a sigh of relief and turned to the other foot. "I'll try not to hurt you," he said, his hand poised above her right leg.

But you will, a voice inside her said. *You will . . .*

She pushed the thought aside. "Go right ahead. I manage pain well."

Don't hurt her. Don't . . . don't hurt her. He repeated the words silently, like a prayer.

Under normal circumstances, Seth knew how to handle a woman as well as he knew how to manage an injured mare. But he felt cold sweat dampen the back of his cotton shirt when he saw the awkward angle of her right ankle. How could she not be screaming in pain?

"I think it's broken, Grace. I'm going to have to stabilize it before we go to the doctor."

"Do what you think best, but I'm not going to the doctor. Once it's set, it'll heal. I'll be fine."

He blinked. Any other woman would be begging for relief—or, he thought wryly, surrendering to his arms like the heroine in one of those *Amisch* romance novels his *mamm* read, waiting to be carried off and rescued.

"You are going to the doctor," he said after a moment. "If money is the issue, I'll pay. You don't have to be all public with the community fund."

He saw a blush suffuse her white cheeks, but he plowed on. "If you're worried about Abel, you know Jacob is fine with him. And if it's simply me—well, too bad. *Der Herr* saw fit to bring me to you today."

"It's all of those things," she said.

He nodded. "Fair enough. Now, hold still if you can. I'm going to slide this piece of wood under your foot and calf." He tried to concentrate on explaining what he was doing and not on her oblique statement—"*It's all of those things.*"

Him included.

Well, that should tell him something. As if it wasn't already obvious that she didn't care a whit for him. She hadn't given him so much as a smile in the six months she'd lived in Pine Creek. He ought to take Jacob's advice and just forget her.

Seth ripped off his shirtsleeve and tore it into strips, then gingerly slid the fabric around the wood and her leg. He steeled himself as he tightened each strip to the fullest, trying not to hear her quiet whimper.

When he was done, he laid his hands on his thighs and fought for breath. He felt winded, as if he'd run a mile in a sodden field. "I'm sorry. So sorry."

She shook her head, her lips white and compressed.

"I'll go get your wagon and bring it round. Then I'll take you to Lockport Hospital. Don't worry, okay?"

He longed to touch her, simply to comfort her. And he almost reached out. Almost.

Then he rose and made himself walk away.

CHAPTER 2

"It's a bad break, Mrs. Wyse." The old doctor was soft-spoken and serious-eyed behind his spectacles.

"Mrs. Beiler," Grace corrected him.

"Oh, excuse me," the *Englisch* man said. "I thought your husband introduced himself as Wyse."

Grace frowned up at Seth, who shrugged and gave her an innocent smile. It wasn't worth the effort to correct the doctor again. She was feeling singularly tired and oddly quivery from the medicine she'd been given for the pain.

"Abel," she whispered.

"He's fine, Grace. Everything will be all right." Seth leaned closer, and she caught the clean scent of him again—teasing, tantalizing—as she felt herself slip thickly into sleep.

She was dreaming. He could tell by the way her black lashes fluttered against her cheeks. She made small, ineffectual movements of her hands, as if she struggled to contain something beyond herself.

"Grace," he whispered. No response.

He leaned over the hospital bed. "Grace," he repeated.

Don't touch her, a voice inside warned him. *Don't touch . . .*

But she was so close, and so obviously troubled. He lifted one of her hands, turned it palm up, and ran the pad of his thumb over it. Her fingers were rough with small needle pricks, marks that testified to hours of hard work, making quilts to sell.

Then her eyes opened and she was staring up at him in confusion.

"Grace, you're at the hospital. They've set and cast your leg and ankle. Do you remember?" He gently laid her hand back on the white sheet.

"What about Abel? He'll be so worried." She made as if to rise, reaching toward the small red Call button on the end of a cord near her head.

"Whoa, wait. I called the barn at home. It's only been three hours. Abel is fine, making gingerbread with *Mamm*."

She sank back down on the pillow.

As she seemed about to drift off again, a nurse bustled in the door—stout, *Englisch*, probably in her late fifties.

"I'm Peggy," she announced. She promptly stepped in front of Seth where he hovered by the bed. "If you'll excuse us, Mr. Wyse, I need to check her vitals."

"Uh, sure." Seth moved back.

The nurse looked him up and down, her gaze pausing on his bare arm. She arched an eyebrow. "I understand you did some first aid yourself, Mr. Wyse?"

Seth flushed when Grace seemed to focus on his arm as well. "Yes. Only a bit."

"I owe you a shirt," Grace mumbled.

The words echoed in his brain, mingling disbelief with resounding promise. It was an intimate thing, the making of a shirt. But when he looked at her pale, beautiful face, he saw only a blank detachment in her gaze. Maybe she was still drugged.

"Forget it," he said. "Let's focus on getting you home instead."

"Yes, you're free to go," Nurse Peggy said. "Dr. Green gave you a walking cast, and you'll soon get used to the feel of it. In the meantime, use the crutches until you get your sea legs. He wants the cast on for at least four weeks. Don't get it wet." She produced a plastic bag with something gray folded inside. "You put this sleeve over your cast when you shower—er, bathe. It's got a little pump seal with it." She handed the bag to Seth and glanced between the two of them. "She'll need help for a few days—getting around, taking some pain meds. Make sure she uses the crutches until she gets used to balancing on the rubber heel. Any problem?"

"No," he said. "No problem at all. She'll have everything she needs." He ignored Grace's glare and turned a full smile on the nurse. "Thank you."

The nurse arched an eyebrow at him as if to say he wasn't so bad, for an *Amisch*. Then she pulled some forms out of a chart for Grace to sign, took the completed forms, and left without another word. Once she had gone, he leaned one hip against the bed and chuckled at Grace.

"What are you laughing at?" she demanded.

"You," he said with a grin. "You need help, and you're going to get it."

Grace leaned on the crutches and tested her weight on the walking cast. She gazed down at it—it was blue, the color of the sky on a midsummer day. The thing felt cumbersome but not too heavy, and much to her surprise, she had very little pain.

Still, she wondered why on earth she had listened to Seth Wyse when he told her that she was coming to the hospital. Because she'd done nothing but listen for years and years, that's why. She had been conditioned to obey.

He pulled the wagon up, then jumped down to help her.

"Back or front?" he asked.

She could barely recall the ride into town. He had laid her on a pile of quilts in the back of the wagon. Now she decided the front would be better—even if it meant sitting next to him and balancing her cast.

"Front."

He lifted her, crutches and all, before she could even catch her breath.

"You weigh nothing, Grace," he said.

"It's not the most polite thing to comment on a lady's weight."

He slid her onto the seat, took her crutches, and deposited them into the bed of the wagon. Then he grinned. "Maybe I'm not the most polite of men."

She stared straight ahead as he climbed up beside

her and took the reins. Of course he was polite. She could hear his kind voice in her mind, talking to people before Meeting, joking with Jacob at some gathering, soothing Abel as he taught him to ride.

The wagon jerked forward and he caught her arm. "Hey, better lean against me with that leg."

"I'm fine."

"Come on. I don't bite, Grace."

She inched a little nearer to him, careful to keep her leg propped on the front board. He encircled her shoulder with a strong arm, edging her flush against his side.

"You can't drive with one hand."

He laughed, a merry, rich sound from deep in his throat. "Grace, I could drive a horse blindfolded and using two toes. Don't worry. And, by the way, I picked that color out, you know."

"What color?"

"The blue. Your cast. I picked it out for you. Could have had green, but I thought it wouldn't go well with your dresses."

She stared down at the blue cast and forced herself to concentrate on the dull throbbing of her leg and the rhythmic sounds of the horse's shoes striking the pavement. "It's vanity to think that way. It . . . it doesn't matter what I wear or how I look."

He pulled her an inch closer. "*Nee*. It doesn't matter, Grace. It doesn't matter at all."

Seth wished the ride would last forever; she fit so perfectly within the circle of his arm. But he knew she was in pain, and more than that, he knew that she would *not* like what he was about to say.

"You know," he began in a matter-of-fact way, "you're going to need help, like the doctor said. Your place is so small, to get around with crutches and all. I thought that maybe you should stay—"

"*Nee.*"

He glanced down at her. "What?"

"*Nee, danki.* Abel and I will be fine together."

He nodded. "Might be a challenge, though, keeping an eye on that boy at the start of a summer's fun." He knew the boy was jumpier than a fly on a string.

She seemed to hesitate, just for a split second. "I— we'll be fine."

Despite her response, he persisted. "You're quilting too, right? You'll need something rigged up so that you can keep that ankle elevated while you work."

"I'll figure it out."

"I have no doubt you can handle everything, Grace. But at least for a day or so—especially while you're taking the pain medicine—why don't you stay at our house? We can keep an eye on Abel, and you can go home feeling better."

She was wavering. He could see it in the set of her fine jawline and the pulse that throbbed in her throat.

"It really would be *gut* for Abel," he added. "I'll take him riding."

This final volley seemed to do the trick. She squared her shoulders beneath his arm. "It's late. I guess—for tonight only. If your *mamm* won't mind."

Mind? She'd be ecstatic. "She will welcome you, Grace.

And we've got plenty of rooms, though you might be more comfortable on the couch."

Grace glanced sideways at him, and he felt his heart rate accelerate at the veiled look.

"Abel—he's been sleeping with me lately. He gets these bouts of anxiety."

Seth smiled. Here was a concrete fact about the beautiful woman: her son was everything to her. "He'll be right with you. I promise."

She pursed her lips. "And are you *gut* at that, Seth Wyse?"

"At what?"

"Making promises?"

He pulled her closer and smiled again. "Only the ones I'm sure I can keep."

She nodded. "We'll see then, won't we?"

He swallowed hard. For the second time in one day, the Widow Beiler had intimated that there was the potential for future encounters between them.

A shirt and a promise. He could live on that.

CHAPTER 3

"Seth Wyse, I'd say you planned this, but for the falling of the stone wall."

In search of a drink of water, Grace was wrangling her crutches toward the sink when she caught the whispered admonishment coming from the pantry. She froze, then realized it was the worst possible thing to do. A moment later Seth and his mother emerged from the pantry room and both stopped still at the sight of her.

"Grace, please forgive me. You must have overheard. I just meant . . ." She trailed off rather helplessly, and Grace couldn't help but notice the flush that stained Seth's cheeks.

Wonderful, she thought. *I'm staying the night at Seth Wyse's house, and his mother thinks he's been pining for me. Esther Zook will probably have it spread all over the community by noon tomorrow.*

Grace couldn't help but grimace when she thought of the gossipy Esther Zook. There were no secrets in a small community, especially when Esther was around. The woman had been trying to create rumors about her since Grace had arrived in Pine Creek six months ago.

"Are you in pain?" Seth took two steps nearer, and she had to resist the urge to bolt.

"I—I'm all right," she stammered.

"What do you need?"

What do I need? Ach, only a better life. Fewer financial worries. More sleep. Help with Abel. An unbroken ankle.

And a man like you.

Her gaze shifted to Mary Wyse, who managed to look both happy and anxious at the same time. Grace couldn't blame her. An older woman, a widow with a child, was not exactly prime potential courting material for a son like Seth Wyse.

Courting material? Where did that come from? It must be the pain medicine.

"Grace, what do you need?" Seth repeated.

"Water," she whispered.

In one fluid motion he lifted her into his arms and strode across the room to deposit her on the couch. "Wait here."

She watched him move toward the kitchen, then saw Abel standing in the doorway. He let out a rare laugh.

"*Mamm*, you're like a *boppli*."

Seth returned with a glass. He handed it to her without comment, but she could see the look of merriment in his eyes. He winked in her direction, then turned to Abel and bent to him where he perched in a comfortable chair. "And you, Abel. What do you want?"

Oh, to know the answer to that question, Grace thought. To understand what the boy wanted, really wanted, what he thought and felt deep inside that mysterious mind *der Herr* had given him. Abel was so unpredictable, so different. She had learned to love these differences, but surely it would take someone else a life-time to adjust to her son.

Nevertheless, Seth and Jacob Wyse had been persis-tent in working to help Abel overcome his fears. Seth, especially, had been teaching him to ride a pony. Grace was truly grateful for the times of respite the two Wyse brothers provided.

Still, she didn't want Seth to get any ideas.

But the man had carried her in his arms twice now—contact her husband had never made with her. Seth had winked and smiled at her in a way that sent a quiver through her. He picked out her cast and knew what color would match her dresses. He—

"I want a puppy," Abel said.

"What?" She craned her neck to see Abel's face better.

"A puppy," Abel and Seth replied in unison, then they both laughed.

Seth snapped his fingers. "I'll bet old Widow Yoder's got a pup or two left from that litter where Jacob got his dog. We could go tomorrow—" He stopped suddenly and whirled to look at Grace. "That is, if you say so, Grace? Or maybe when you're feeling better?"

Abel was already flapping his arms in delight and rushing toward her. He halted within an inch of the couch. "*Ach*, can we, *Mamm*? Huh? Puppy! Puppy! Puppy!"

Grace squeezed a hand across her forehead and closed her eyes. A puppy? She had her hands full with Abel and work and trying to make ends meet. How could she possibly deal with a puppy?

She felt a slight touch on her uninjured leg and

looked up to find Seth sitting on the end of the couch. "Grace, I'm sorry," he muttered. "I didn't stop to think—well, that he would take me so literally when I asked what he wanted. I was really asking what he wanted to drink, you know?"

Abel was now spinning about the room, his head tilted upward, unaware of their talk. Of course Seth wouldn't understand how literal Abel could be. She breathed a deep sigh and cast an eye to where Mary Wyse had busied herself at the sink, her back turned.

"Look, if it'll give him that much joy, he can have the pup. I've always wanted him to have a dog, but my husband—I mean, Silas—"

"Wouldn't allow it?" Seth said.

She nodded but didn't elaborate, and to her relief he didn't press her for anything further. "Still, you should have asked me first. It's a big responsibility, and it'll fall on me."

"I'll help you."

She covered her face with both hands and shook her head. No. She was not going to let him help. She should have gone home tonight, away from Seth Wyse and his blue eyes and his easiness with life. He had no idea how different her world was—or how difficult.

"Grace, please?" he whispered. "Let me help. I promise I won't push you. Just friends. How about it?"

She lifted her face and took in his earnest expression. It might be good to have a friend—a strong friend, someone she could lean on. It would be good for Abel too.

She lifted her hand from her lap and held it out to him. "Just friends," she said clearly.

He shook her hand in a warm grasp, then let her go. "Just friends."

Seth paced the confines of his room in the still darkness of the summer's night. He was wearing his loose painting shirt and black pants, and his suspenders hung about his hips, tapping him every time he turned. He was full of restless energy, knowing that Grace slept a floor beneath him. Maybe he could make some excuse to check on her.

What am I, fifteen? Do I want to go down and get a bedtime drink of water? Tuck her in? Pretend I heard a noise or something?

Just stop and paint! And quit being so narrisch!

He went to stand before the canvas, running a fan brush hard against his thumb and forefinger. There was a soft knock at the door and he turned, his heart in his throat at the crazy notion that it might be Grace.

"*Kumme* in."

It was his *daed*. Samuel Wyse was as tall as his sons and had clear, knowing, green eyes in a face prematurely craggy from a lifetime of sun and wind.

Seth laid the brush aside and looked at his father expectantly. "What's the matter, *Daed*? It's late to be up."

His father smiled and went to sit on the edge of Seth's bed. "But you're up, *sohn*. I heard you pacing like a panther in here."

Seth grimaced. "Sorry."

Samuel waved a large hand in dismissal. "*Nee*. I'm worried about you—and your *mamm* frets too."

"Please, don't. I haven't meant to trouble you these last months with my, ah, interest in Grace Beiler."

His *daed* laughed gently. "I think it goes a bit beyond *interest*, don't you?"

"I don't know. I gave my word tonight to be her friend, to stop pushing for something more."

"Can you do that, Seth? Lay aside something you're passionate about?"

Seth caught his father's eye. "Why do I think we're talking about more than Grace here?"

His father stroked his beard. "I have to tell you something, Seth. I heard tonight that over in Elk Valley, an *Amisch* community shunned a man because he was doing pen-and-ink drawings of nature and the like."

Seth gazed briefly at the half-finished forest scene on the easel. A knot twisted in his gut. "Oh."

"You know we love you, Seth," his father went on quietly. "We've hidden this art of yours from the community for years—to keep the joy you've had in it this long. But I wonder what Grace Beiler would say about this passion of yours? Maybe there's more than just a floor that separates the two of you. She may not understand."

Seth looked hard at his father. "Are you saying now, after all this time, that I should give up my art, or tell the bishop?"

"I don't know, *sohn*. That's your decision as a man. I'm just pointing out that there's much more to you than Seth Wyse the skirt chaser." His father smiled, then grew serious. "And maybe, *sohn*, there's also more to Grace Beiler than meets the eye."

Seth picked the brush back up with slow intent. "Then I still have a lot to learn in life."

"We all do, Seth—always learning, always growing closer to *der Herr*. That is where you will find your wisdom."

"Thanks, *Daed*." Seth crossed the room as his father rose from the bed. He hugged the older man tightly and smiled when his *daed* ruffled his hair like he did when he was a kid. Then the door closed with a quiet click and Seth turned back to the painting.

His eyes burned, and the image on the canvas wavered in front of him. How could he survive without his art? But could it drive Grace away if she knew? And what about his *mamm* and *daed*—so honest, so faithful. He had let them harbor a lie all this time. Suppose Bishop Loftus found out and took a cue from the Elk Valley community? What had seemed like an innocent family secret had the potential to hurt so many.

He clenched the brush in his hand, closed his eyes, and started to pray.

CHAPTER 4

"A re you sleeping, Mama?" Abel's voice was hushed in the semi-dark living room. Mary Wyse had left a single lamp burning low on the kitchen table, a warm and comforting glow. Grace sat up a bit to look at her *sohn*.

"I'm *supposed* to be sleeping." She laughed softly. "Are you having trouble?"

"*Nee*." The child's voice was muffled. "I was thinking how nice it is here—like home, kinda."

Grace swallowed. *Like home.*

The small house that she and Abel had moved to six months ago was a sanctuary, certainly. But home? All she had of home were teasing memories: her parents, her brothers, her little sister, Violet, who had just turned eight when Grace left home. She was nearly grown by now, probably looking for a husband and family of her own.

Once she'd married Silas, he had forbidden any contact with her family. They were still neighbors, but they might as well have lived a thousand miles away. Silas kept her on a short leash, and her *mamm* and *daed* avoided any contact. Maybe they felt guilty for what they had done, or maybe they feared Silas would change his mind and call in their debts. Whatever the case, she rarely saw them except at a distance, and they kept her brothers and sister away from her as well. Anything she knew about the family came to her secondhand.

She sighed faintly, then refocused on the moment. "Do you want me to tell you a story, *sohn*?"

She heard the smile in Abel's voice. "*Nee, Mamm.* I'll tell you one, about a handsome prince. Maybe he looks like Seth . . ."

Grace smiled wryly and settled back to hear her son's tale. It seemed that no one was immune to the visible charms of Seth Wyse.

Violet Raber yawned and crawled with stiff weariness from the back of the van. Rock music blared from the stereo, shattering the predawn peace.

"Thanks for the ride, Tommy." She reached into her satchel for some money to pay the teenage neighbor who'd driven her from Ohio to Pine Creek, Pennsylvania.

"Hey, I'll only take enough for gas, all right?" He grinned at her, crooked teeth in an honest face. "So, you got family here?"

"Distant cousins," she answered vaguely. "Haven't seen them in years." She handed him the money, thanked him, then shut the van door against the noise of the music and adjusted her *kapp*.

Tommy waved and roared away. When he was gone, Violet stood in the darkness and blinked until her eyes adjusted to the inky light. An *Amisch* man she and

Tommy had passed directed her here, but the small house seemed lifeless. Grace and her son—what was his name? Adam? Abe?—could very well be asleep at this hour. She yawned again and made her way to the small run of steps.

She knocked. No answer.

She tried the door. It was locked.

"Well," she muttered aloud, "maybe she's moved somewhere else."

Within a month of Silas Beiler's death, Grace had packed up and left Middle Hollow without a word to anyone. Rumor was that she had gone to the *Amisch* community of Pine Creek, Pennsylvania, where their King relatives lived, but no one seemed to know for sure. A few weeks later both *Mamm* and *Daed* died when a truck came over a hill and rear-ended their buggy. But when Violet wrote to Grace in care of Pine Creek General Delivery, the letter was returned undelivered.

It was a long shot, coming here. And yet the local *Amisch* man seemed to know who Grace was—the young widow from Ohio with a little boy in tow.

Violet trudged off the porch and decided to walk the mile or two up to the big farm they passed on the road coming in. It was nearly daybreak. Somebody there was bound to be up, and maybe they knew something more about Grace.

With weary determination she headed back toward the hulking shadows of great barns. Maybe she'd find a place to rest for a moment, as well as news of her sister.

Seth was up earlier than usual. A roan, a gelding, had a lame leg, and in the bustle of the previous day with Grace, he hadn't had time to give it the attention it needed. Jacob had probably tended to the horse, but he needed to be sure—not to mention the fact that he hoped Grace might be an early riser too.

He slid his suspenders into place over his light blue work shirt and eased quietly down the hall. Downstairs, in the dim lamplight, Seth could see Abel's dark head pillowed against his mother's breast as the two snuggled close on the couch. He stood for a moment gazing down at the two of them and then, not wanting to be caught staring, tiptoed onto the front porch and pulled on his boots.

Dawn was breaking just over the horizon, and the morning was cool and misty. He inhaled a deep breath of clear summer air, then did a double take. There, dozing in one of the generous whitewashed rockers on the front porch, sat Grace.

Seth looked back over his shoulder toward the front door. Was he losing his mind? Was he so addled with the idea of Grace Beiler that he was seeing double? Before he had a chance to sort it all out, the apparition opened her eyes and blinked up at him. "Hello."

He frowned down at her. "And who might you be?"

"Violet," she said, her voice rusty with sleep. "Violet Raber. Forgive me for intruding. I'm looking for my sister."

Seth stooped down next to her chair. "Your sister?"

The girl nodded. "Mm-hmm—Grace Beiler."

"Grace is your sister?"

The girl seemed to become fully awake in that moment and sat bolt upright in the chair. "Do you know her? Do you know where she is?"

"She's sleeping," he said finally. "Right inside, in fact. She broke her ankle yesterday, and I brought her here to rest and have some help."

The girl scrambled to her feet and Seth rose as well. It really was amazing how much this sister of Grace's looked like the woman he had his heart set on. Except for the eyes. Grace's were the color of a purple pansy; this sister's eyes were blue as the sea.

Still, he wasn't about to let anyone disturb Grace's sleep, sister or not.

"Why not walk down to the barn with me for a bit? Your sister really does need her sleep. We'll get acquainted, and then you can talk to her when she wakes up."

"All right." She glanced at the door behind him. "Just until she wakes, then."

Grace woke to a persistent tweaking of her nose.

"Sqwoosh. Sqwoosh. Sqwoosh." The sounds matched the tiny pinches on her nostrils. She lifted her eyelids to see Abel staring with solemnity down at her while he repeatedly felt her nose.

"Good morning," she said, stifling a yawn.

"Why do we have holes in our noses, *Mamm*?"

"So air can get in and out."

"Why do you tell me not to pick my nose?"

Grace sighed faintly. "Because it's rude."

He let go of her nose. "Okay. I'm hungry."

Grace made to rise, but pain shot through her. She was reaching for her crutches when she heard the floor squeak. Mary Wyse, no doubt tiptoeing into the kitchen so as not to wake her.

"It's all right," Grace called from the couch. She struggled to a sitting position as Abel slid onto the floor in a curled-up pile. "I'm awake."

"*Ach, gut.*" Mary poked her head around the door post. "What would you like for breakfast? What does Abel like special?" Grace grasped her crutches and Mary waved her back down. "Grace, *sei so gut.* Sit, sit. Abel's got the right idea."

Grace looked at the limp body of her son and was grateful for the other woman's understanding of Abel's odd posture. It was part of his autism—assuming strange poses that were supposedly comforting to him but looked odd enough to the untrained eye.

"Thanks, but we don't want to be any trouble. Maybe I could make it home on my crutches."

Mary set the lamp on a nearby table and put her hands on her hips. "Grace, really, let us help you. We—"

The squeaking of the front screen door made her pause, and Grace followed her gaze as Seth entered, holding the hand of a beautiful young girl. For one sweeping moment, Grace felt a strange tightening in her chest, then she forced herself to smile.

Friends. They were just friends. So this must be some new *Amisch* girl he'd picked up. Knowing Seth's charm, he probably found her under a cabbage leaf in the morning dew. She tried to tamp down the sarcasm and act as if it didn't matter. And then suddenly the girl was

rushing to her in a flurry of beauty and color and somehow knew her name.

Seth watched the two women embrace. He had no
idea about Grace's family of origin, and what he'd
been able to glean from Violet was nothing concrete.
But it made him extremely happy for Grace's sake
to see some connection. She was always so reserved
about her past. She'd rarely spoken to him about anything more significant than the weather or the horses
or the phases of the moon. Never about anything
personal.

Abel, on the other hand, had told him things that
sent a chill through Seth's heart.

Seth looked around for Abel, who had scuttled away
under a side table, scrunching down, looking furtively
at his mother.

Seth slid out of his work boots and went to where the
little boy hid.

"Do you know who that is, Abel?" he asked in a soft
voice.

"*Nee*," Abel whispered. "It's not my *mamm*."

"No, of course not," Seth agreed. *Even though I
thought the same thing until the girl opened her eyes.* "I
think it's your *aenti* Violet. Why not go over and say
hiya?"

"*Jah*," Grace called. "*Kumme*, Abel, meet my little
sister, Violet."

Violet turned her attention to her tentative nephew.

She held out a hand. "Hello, Abel. I'm very glad to meet you."

"You never met him?" Seth asked in a low voice. "How can that be?"

Violet shrugged. "Ask my big sister."

CHAPTER 5

I appreciate your time and trouble, Seth."

"It's all right."

As soon as they reached the house, Abel had dragged Violet inside to show her around, leaving Grace to stand, one-footed and awkward, outside on the stoop with Seth.

She swallowed. "And *danki* for bringing Violet to me."

"I'm surprised she hasn't visited you before. You've been here six months."

"I haven't seen her for a long time."

"I gathered that," he said. "What I don't understand is why."

Grace shrugged. "It's complicated."

Seth desperately wanted to reach out to her, but she had made it clear that she would not welcome any such overture. She had absolutely insisted on being brought home, citing Violet as ample and able help.

"Good day, then," she said. "And give my thanks to your *mamm*."

"I will." He was about to say something more,

anything to keep her talking, but she hobbled inside and closed the door.

Seth was still nursing his disappointment when he drove up toward the farm and saw a stranger leading his horse to drink in one of the troughs alongside the fence. The man was a contradiction—*Amisch* haircut, *Englisch* clothes. But what really attracted Seth's attention was the man's saddle and the simple, unmistakable brown box art kit that hung there.

Seth drew rein on the wagon, set the brake, and jumped down.

"Hiya," he said. "Passing through?"

The man was tall and lean with sandy hair and brown eyes. He glanced between Seth and the trough and nodded. "Hope you don't mind about the water. You gotta keep a horse well watered."

"Help yourself." Seth waved away his concern, then drew a deep breath. "You from Elk Valley?"

The stranger snorted. "I should have known better. Bad news travels fast."

Seth reached out a hand to stop him from bolting. "Look, I'm Seth Wyse, and *jah*, news came around that an artist in Elk Valley was shunned for his work. I saw your materials box and wondered—"

But the stranger was now regarding him with speculation and something akin to respect. "You . . . you said 'my work'?"

Seth shrugged. "Of course it's your work—takes time and talent, doesn't it? God-given talent?"

The stranger extended a hand. "I'm Gabe Loftus, and I'd say you know a thing or two about art."

"Maybe."

"Well, don't let the community find out, nor the bishop, or you'll be out on your ear like me."

"You know our bishop? His name is Loftus too."

"I suppose we're probably kin somewhere back down the road," Gabe said. "I don't know yours; I just know what bishops can do."

Seth sighed. "*Jah*, I get it. Where you headed to? Are you hungry?"

Gabe backed his horse away from the trough. "*Nee*, but thanks all the same. I'm going over to Pleasant Valley. I've got some *Englisch* family there. Figured I'd start over, somehow."

"Do you have anything with you?" Seth asked on impulse. "Any of your work?"

Gabe gave him a gap-toothed smile. "Maybe."

"I'd like to see it, maybe buy something—help a stranger on his way."

Gabe shook his head. "If anyone finds out, you'll be—"

"Let me worry about that."

Gabe shrugged and went to his saddle. He slid a cardboard tube from beneath his gear, and the two men went to lean against the fence while the horses grazed.

"I don't know if it's any *gut*, really." Gabe unrolled a sheaf of drawings from the tube. Seth's eyes caught on the elegant strokes of amazingly lifelike renderings: a woman's face in profile, a rabbit poised, a coyote in the winter snow.

"These are excellent," Seth said. "You're really good." He felt tears prick the backs of his eyes. Here was kinship, understanding. For a moment his father's warnings echoed in his mind, but they couldn't dampen the enthusiasm he felt in another artist's presence.

Then he came to a small, intricate drawing of a quilt, half-finished. The loose threads of the quilt reached out to touch both the quilters and others in the room, even a grumpy-looking old man sitting in a corner. There was a distinct air of hope about the drawing that reminded him of Grace.

"I don't know why I've kept that," Gabe confided. "Probably one of my first, but not my best. The shading's off."

"It's wonderful. Why the threads, though?"

"I was trying to make a statement, I guess—that all of us, good and bad, are part of life's quilt. Sounds silly, I suppose."

"I'll take it," Seth said. "How much do you want?" He handed back the other drawings carefully.

Gabe laughed, a sound of joy released. "I have no idea. Ten dollars?"

Seth reached into his satchel. "Ten times that. This makes me feel especially *gut*."

Gabe held up his hands in protest, but Seth pressed the bills into his palm, then clasped his hand in a gesture of goodwill. "If I'm ever in Pleasant Valley, I'll look you up—artist."

Gabe shook his head as he pocketed the money and mounted his horse. "Thanks," Gabe said. "And not just for the sale."

Seth waved the thin drawing he held at him. "*Danki* yourself. Have a *gut* trip."

Seth watched him ride away, then slowly went back

to the wagon and climbed onto the seat. He rolled the small drawing up and held it carefully, driving with one hand.

He felt good—renewed, hopeful, as if *der Herr* had given him a slender view of the future, of hopes and dreams fulfilled. And whatever the bishop might say, he prayed that Gabe Loftus would begin a blessed new life.

CHAPTER 6

By breakfast the next morning, Grace had suffered through a sleepless night, trying to digest the news her sister brought: both parents dead, two brothers who left the *Amisch* life, the loss of the family farm. It was too much to take in. How could she have been so close and yet so isolated?

"But that's not all," Violet said.

Grace had only to look into her sister's eyes to grasp her meaning.

"God help us," she breathed. "Not Tobias."

Tobias Beiler had been a wavering shadow in the background of Grace's married life to his brother, Silas. Younger, stronger, with brown hair rather than gray, Tobias nevertheless was cut from the same cloth as his older brother. All too vividly she remembered the look in his eyes, the leering, threatening expression.

"Do you really think he might come here?"

Violet bit her lip. "If I found you, he can find you too. He was in Middle Hollow asking a lot of questions right before I left." She narrowed her eyes. "What does he want with you?"

Grace knew but kept quiet. She should have realized he wouldn't give up so easily.

Then, as if her thoughts had summoned him, she heard a heavy step on the porch, an insistent pounding on the front door.

Violet went to the window and peered out. "He's here!"

"Take Abel and go," Grace said. "Out the back door. Go to Seth's. Now!"

"I won't leave you," Violet protested.

"He won't hurt me." Grace's voice betrayed her uncertainty. But still she pushed Violet in the direction of Abel's room. "Get my son, please. Take him to Seth's, and don't let him come back. Go now!"

Violet darted into Abel's room, picked up the sleepy boy, and dashed out the back door. Only when she saw them fleeing across the field toward the Wyse farm did Grace turn back.

The front door hung open. Tobias stood in the kitchen doorway with a satchel slung over his shoulder, looking as gray and gaunt as Silas himself. "So, sweet sister-in-law, I've been waiting quite awhile for this." Tobias advanced on her. "It took me some time to track you down. You really didn't think you could run from me forever, did you?"

When she didn't respond, he inched nearer. "*Jah*, here we are, Grace, and just in time, right? Six months since my brother died. I see no man around . . ."

He pulled a sheaf of papers from his bag and slapped them down onto the kitchen table. "Recognize this, Grace? My brother's will? Isn't that what he wrote— that you must always be yoked under the burden of a man to keep you in line? Six months he gave you, and if you are not married, I get it all. Silas's house, the farm, the money—*ach*, and the brat too."

"Take the money," she breathed. "Take the farm. I'll sign it all over to you. I don't want it. Just take it and go. But leave Abel out of it."

Tobias clutched her arm. "*Nee*, sweet Grace. Because if I have the boy, you will do anything I want to get him back. Anything. Won't you?"

"Let her go." Seth kept his voice level, though he longed to grab the intruder by the throat.

The man turned. "Ah, the hero." He kept his hold on Grace and pulled her around in front of him. One crutch clattered to the floor.

It was not the *Amisch* way to lay hands on another. Seth tried to hold on to that thought while he considered how satisfying it would be to break the man's arms.

"So, hero, are you her husband?"

"*Nee*," Seth said.

"Then you can leave." He looked down at Grace. "Tell him to go. This doesn't concern him."

Seth saw her eyes dart toward a sheaf of papers on the small kitchen table. He walked with deliberate slowness to the table and flipped idly through the documents.

"Why does it matter whether or not I'm her husband?" He forced himself to keep his voice calm.

The other man snickered. "My brother, Grace's poor deceased husband, was nothing if not thoughtful, wasn't he, Grace? And his *fraa* here was compliant. She signed away her rights to Abel and to all the inheritance money if my brother should have an untimely death and she had not remarried in six months. My *gut bruder* thought that a married state would be best for her, to keep her from sin. *Jah*, Grace? The six months is up tomorrow at noon."

She twisted in his grasp and Seth gritted his teeth. He spoke softly to Grace. "Is this true?"

She nodded.

It was all he needed.

The words broke from his lips. "Well then, you have a problem—because Grace and I are due to be married. Tomorrow. At eleven o'clock."

Tobias was gone.

When her shaking subsided, Grace did what she had always trained herself to do: she focused not on the emotion of the moment but on the issue that needed to be resolved. "Where is Abel?" she asked Seth.

"At the farm. He's fine. Jacob and Violet are with him. Did he . . . hurt you?"

Grace shook her head. Her eyes darted around the small house, scanning the few belongings she possessed, wondering what she should take with her when she fled. She glanced briefly at Seth. "*Sei so gut*. Bring Abel back. If I hurry in gathering our things, we can be gone within the hour. I want to make *gut* time before it gets dark. Violet doesn't have to come."

"What? Where are you going? *Kumme* sit down, your hands are trembling."

He pulled out a chair at the table and she ignored

him, brushing past his arm on her crutches to reach for a basket on the floor. "*Danki* for the marriage ploy. I will pack now and take Abel with me. We can be far into the mountains before tomorrow."

He said nothing. She continued hobbling around the kitchen, gathering pots and pans and silverware until it was obvious he was waiting for her undivided attention.

At last she turned to find him staring at her, his eyes dark blue and impassioned. "It was no ploy, Grace. I will marry you."

She allowed herself a brief, sad smile. "You don't understand. You are young. You see me on the surface, but you really know nothing about me."

He frowned at her, one side of his handsome mouth lifted. She dropped her gaze and began to mentally sort through Abel's clothes.

"Hey," he said, "exactly how long have you been running from this man?"

She stiffened her spine. "My husband died last winter in an ice fishing accident."

"And then you came here, right? For a new start? Or was it to get away from the *bruder*-in-law?"

"You speak of it all so glibly. How can you possibly understand?"

"I can't. So tell me."

Tell him? Where would she possibly start? How could she explain any of it in a way that anyone else could understand? Especially another man.

"Grace?"

She snapped back to awareness. "I thank you for

your kindness to me, and to Abel. But I cannot say more. I must leave. Immediately."

"Marry me, Grace."

She took in a stuttering breath. "Why?"

He moved very close to her, so close that she caught the fresh scent of hay and paint and pine. "I may be younger than you in years. I may think you're beautiful, *jah*, and may have grown attached to your *sohn*. But the real answer to your 'why' is that I understand horses."

She stared into his eyes and felt something like static electricity arc between them, touching him, touching her. Then she came to herself and realized what he'd said.

"Horses?"

"Yep. Horses are creatures that must be discerned, felt through the heart and the mind. If not, you'll never respect them for the mystery, the majesty of their souls."

"And you think I'm like a horse?" She didn't know whether to be flattered or insulted, but one thing she did know: they were wasting time. "All this talk is nonsense, Seth Wyse. We cannot possibly marry."

He smiled in pleasure at her use of his name. "Yes, exactly like a horse. I think I have to read you like a horse, by instinct. And my instincts say that you know you cannot outrun someone as evil as this man. Not when he's got the law on his side. So let me ask you properly."

He caught her hand. "Grace, will you do me the honor of becoming my wife? My flaws aside, my age not thought of, and with the understanding that we shall be man and wife in name only for as long as you choose."

She swallowed hard, feeling as if she were poised on the edge of a high cliff, toes pointed outward, arms open, ready to fly. She thought of Abel and his future and then heard her own voice like an echo on the wind.

"*Jah.*"

CHAPTER 7

I thought I told you not to do anything crazy." Jacob stood with his hands on his hips, looking much like their *daed* for a moment.

Seth led Grace's horse, Amy, into a stall and gave her some feed. He'd driven Grace's buggy over with his horse, Star Bright, trailing behind on a lead. Grace had been anxious to find Abel and Violet and talk to them. Seth could see them now, some distance outside the barn, Grace's slight form bent over her crutches as she spoke with an earnest expression to her son. Violet stood away from them, examining a blooming red rosebush.

"You? Talking to me about crazy?" Seth grinned. "You married Lilly on a whim and it all worked out. Why shouldn't it for me too?"

"That was different."

"How?"

"I don't know, but it was different. It was God at work. This . . . this is *you* at work."

"I think I resent that."

"Well, don't. That woman hasn't wanted anything to do with you, and now some crisis has her back against

a wall and suddenly, for some reason, she's marrying you."

"I know." Seth shrugged with a quick smile. "I'll pray
about it."

"Why is she agreeing?"

Seth explained as much as he knew, and Jacob finally
nodded. "It sounds like you did the right thing, protecting her and Abel, but there might be another way,
a legal way."

"An *Englischer's* law to aid an Amish woman? I don't
think so."

"Maybe the bishop could do something," Jacob persisted. "Let him at least look at those papers you've got."

"Why, Jacob? Why are you, above all people, against
this? You know it's what I've wanted—I can't sleep half
the time for thinking of her."

"Seth, you're my best friend and my only brother. I
love you. But you're like the *kinner*, grabbing for sweets.
You think you've got what you've wanted, but there's
more to a woman than how she looks. And I have a
feeling that the one standing outside is deep water."

"Then I'll have fun drowning."

"You don't get it."

Seth stepped closer to his brother, his face now serious. "Look, Jacob, I know it sounds *narrisch*, but I've
never wanted anything as much as I want Grace Beiler.
Something about her calls to my heart." He turned
away and felt Jacob's hand on his shoulder.

"Seth, I'll support whatever you do. You helped me
with Lilly and I can try to do the same for you. So what's
next?"

Seth turned back to look him in the eye. "We go to the bishop."

"That should be . . . interesting."

Seth cuffed his *bruder* lightly on the shoulder. "*Painful* is more the word."

They both laughed, then Seth spoke. "*Danki,* Jacob. I know I'm going to need your help." He turned to look out at Grace and Abel.

"Well, you've got it, little *bruder.* Anytime."

"*Gut.* Will you send Violet in to talk to *Mamm* or something?"

"No problem."

Seth nodded thanks, but his mind was on the woman in black outside and the small boy by her side.

Tobias Beiler drove his horse blindly and entered Lockport with his whip drawn and his mind in turmoil. He jumped out and looped the reins over the post in front of Eshler's Bed and Breakfast. He stroked down his graying beard, took a deep breath, and approached the carved wooden reception counter.

"Morning," he said in a soft voice.

He felt the *Amisch* woman's eyes study him for a moment before she replied, and he met her gaze squarely.

"Hello. I'm Lillian Eshler. May I help you?"

He cleared his throat. "Here for a wedding. I need a room."

For a moment she hesitated. Tobias tried to rearrange his face into a more pleasing expression. Over the years he had been told that he was growing to look more and more like his brother, Silas, whose features had hardened with age into something fierce, angry, and immovable.

"Booked up, are you?" He reached for his pocket-book, which bulged with cash, and casually flashed the money. "Anything you've got will do."

"*Nee*, sorry," she said. "We're full."

He scowled at her and she retreated a step, as if he might do her violence. Then he turned and slammed out of the place. It was probably better to stay at an *Englischer's* in any case. He planned to be around for a while, wedding or no wedding. He had no intention of letting Grace—or his brother's estate—slip from his grasp so easily.

Grace bent to peer carefully into the eyes of her son. "Abel, you know Seth Wyse?"

"Of course." The boy shifted restlessly.

"Abel, Seth Wyse has asked me—that is, us—to marry him."

"What about the bad man? Uncle Tobias?"

"He will go away."

"What do you mean 'us' to marry Seth?"

Grace smiled gently. "He wants us to become his family. Both of us. If you say *nee*, then I will say *nee* as well."

"I like Seth. Do you?" Abel's eyes were intent now, locked on her own. She resisted the urge to look away.

"Abel, I think he is a good man."

The boy nodded. "But do you like him?"

"I want to like him. I will like him when I get to know him better. I—we—will get to know each other more after we are married."

Abel shrugged. "Okay."

Grace drew a deep breath and straightened, but then he caught her hand. "*Mamm*, will Seth be like *Fater* was?"

"No," she said firmly. "Nothing like *Fater*."

And she prayed it would be so.

Violet gave a sidelong glance at her sister as Abel ambled away. "It sounded like that went well."

"So it would seem," Grace said with a sigh.

Violet snapped her fingers under her sister's nose. "Grace, think. This is not Silas Beiler, not by a long shot. Think how lucky you are to have found someone who loves you and wants to cherish you and—"

"You don't know that."

Violet blew out a frustrated breath. "I've got eyes, don't I? I can't imagine what it would feel like to have a man look at you the way Seth does."

Grace turned to her. "Violet, tell me true and quick. Are you, well, are you attracted to him?"

Violet couldn't suppress the giggle of surprise that bubbled up in her throat. "Grace, what woman wouldn't be? But no, sweet sister, I do not want him. He's all yours."

CHAPTER 8

When a widow or widower remarried, there was no need to wait for the usual season of weddings, October through December. But Seth was pretty sure that no widow had ever decided on a marriage with such haste. He squeezed Grace's hand as they mounted the steps to the bishop's house.

Bishop Loftus was a wizened old man with a sharp wit and an even sharper tongue. There was no telling what he might say in any given circumstance, and there was always the chance that he might not even give approval to Seth's scheme. Still, as Seth fingered the sheaf of legal papers in one hand, he felt fairly confident that all would go well.

Ellie Loftus, the bishop's *fraa*, opened the door to them with a kind smile. She was a straight-backed, small woman who had the kind of eyes that said they'd seen a world of things, and not all good, but still accepted with compassion and empathy.

"Grace, Seth, *sei so gut*, *kumme* in. How's your leg— Esther Zook told me about the wall and your broken ankle. Where's little Abel?"

"Uh, with Jacob. We were hoping that the bishop was around," Seth said.

"Well, *kumme* in and sit and I'll fetch him." She leaned forward conspiratorially. "He's in a bit of a bad mood. Some woodworking he was doing for the upstairs didn't turn out well."

"Ach," Seth murmured. His gut twisted, but he glanced down into Grace's eyes and tried to smile at her with reassurance. She didn't smile back. They perched on the rather stiff sofa that Ellie indicated and waited while she hollered up the steps in Pennsylvania Dutch for her husband. His cantankerous reply made Seth tug at his shirt collar.

Loud steps sounded on the stairs as the bishop clumped down in his work boots. If he was surprised to see Seth and Grace sitting together in his living room, he didn't show it. The old man merely dropped into a chair facing them and raised a gray eyebrow.

"Well?"

"I'll make lemonade," Ellie murmured, disappearing into the kitchen.

Seth cleared his throat. "We've come about getting married."

"Humph," the bishop grunted.

"Tomorrow. At eleven. If you're not busy."

Bishop Loftus leaned back in his chair. "I'm not busy."

Seth smiled. Maybe this was going to be easy. "Then if you consent, we can—"

"Did I say I consented?"

"Nee, but—"

The bishop shifted the full force of his gaze to Grace. "Seth Wyse is a runaround. He's kissed more girls in this county and the next than I would care to count. He's wild, restless, and has had his eyes on you since you moved here, Grace Beiler. And you have wanted nothing to do with him. So why should I give consent?"

Seth sensed Grace straighten a bit by his side and felt a certain pride in her character, despite the words that came forth from her lips.

"I have no desire to marry him, Bishop Loftus, nor any other man. My first husband was enough for a lifetime. But I was young and foolish when I married. I signed papers."

She indicated the folder in Seth's hand. Seth extended the documents, but the bishop waved them away.

Grace went on. "I could lose Abel to an evil man if I do not marry Seth Wyse. He has offered. I understand his faults. I have plenty of faults of my own. I will do my best to be a *gut* wife to him for saving my son."

The bishop stroked his long gray beard. "Hmm. Self-sacrifice is a poor foundation to marry upon. It's an even sadder substitute for love."

Grace did not respond, and Seth held his breath in the silence.

Finally the bishop nodded. "Very well. Eleven o'clock tomorrow. I will prepare a suitable sermon for the both of you. Ellie?" He turned and hollered in the direction of the kitchen. "Ellie? Where's that lemonade? You've got to congratulate these two—they're going to be married."

Seth gently steered Grace and Abel ahead of him and into his home while Violet followed behind. The living room windows were open and a light breeze played across the wood floors and simple furnishings. The smell of freshly brewing tea and baking molasses cookies filled the air.

His *daed*, Samuel, was seated at the kitchen table reading *The Budget*. His *mamm* turned from the stove. Seth shepherded Grace and Abel forward.

"*Mamm, Daed*, the wid—I mean, Grace—has done me the honor of accepting my proposal of marriage, and Abel has also given his consent. We've been to the bishop's, and . . . well, we're to marry tomorrow at eleven o'clock."

There was a distinct moment of silence while his *daed* put down the newspaper and stared at him. His *mamm* froze, a wooden spoon in hand.

"They're thinking it's strange," Abel said clearly, and Seth half laughed, putting his hand on the boy's shoulder. He sensed Grace tense even further while Violet fidgeted beside her.

His *daed* cleared his throat. "Well, that's . . . fine, *sohn*." He rose slowly from the table and looked at his wife. "Isn't that fine, Mary?"

His *mamm* burst into a smile, as if released from a spell. "*Jah*, fine! Grace, Abel—we welcome you. And, Violet, you too, of course. How *wunderbaar* that you can be here to help your sister prepare." She put down her spoon and came around the table to pull mother and son into her arms, then she hugged Violet and embraced Seth but drew back to look up at him. "*Ach*, Seth, there's so much to do. I hardly know where to begin."

"We don't want to be any bother," Grace said quickly.

Mary Wyse laughed. "A wedding is no bother; it's a time for celebration. What will you wear, Grace?"

Although the *Amisch* of their community did not wear anything special for weddings, blue was traditionally favored by the bride.

"I'm not quite sure yet. I'll go through my dresses."

"What will I wear, *Mamm*?" Abel asked.

Grace looked at her son rather helplessly, and Seth spoke up. "Jacob and I will take care of you, Abel. Black coat, tie, shiny boots."

The boy cut a glance in his *mamm's* direction. "I don't like a tie around my neck."

"No tie then," Seth assured him.

"I don't much care for a tie either," Samuel Wyse said with a smile. "But a new daughter-in-law and a *kinskind* are a double blessing."

Grace tried to relax. Everyone was kind, but the silent questions reverberated through her brain: What was she doing? Why would Seth make a lifetime commitment to help her? How was it really going to be for Abel? And the most troubling question of all: How in the world was she going to live with the most attractive man she'd ever seen without losing her heart?

She had struggled to avoid Seth, with his kind words and gentle acts of thoughtfulness. He made no effort to hide the fact that he was infatuated with her, but she also knew that he'd be disappointed once the proverbial candy wrapper had been peeled away. She suddenly felt light-headed, and Mary Wyse must have noticed because she led Grace to the couch and helped her settle among the cushions.

"Sit down and rest. You must be exhausted. I know that sudden change always makes me feel like I've got my bonnet blown off and a wind up my skirt."

Grace couldn't help but smile at the kind woman's talk. She wasn't used to talking to another mature *Amisch* woman, at least not idle talk. She was half afraid her in-laws might see her as some sodden cat that Seth dragged home and felt sorry for.

But she had to stop thinking that way. She had to believe in herself, to believe that *Gott* had made her worthwhile, no matter what was in her past.

She felt Abel come and cuddle next to her side and she stroked his hair. He did not especially like to be touched unless he wanted it. He must be nervous or he wouldn't come this close.

She was tired, so tired. She wanted to close her eyes and go to sleep right where she was, to let the ground swallow her up and moss grow over her.

Grace let her weary gaze roam discreetly over her prospective husband. He so closely resembled her childish fantasy of what the future should hold. Now, suddenly, this broad-shouldered, lean-hipped man was going to be with her forever.

What on earth had she gotten herself into?

Seth saw Grace and Abel and Violet home after a filling, spontaneous celebratory dinner of stuffed meat loaf, mashed potatoes, and new asparagus shoots.

Abel retreated into his bedroom with Violet for company. While his mother and Grace and Violet were making plans, Seth had slipped away and set the front door back on its hinges.

Now he shut the door behind them. "I don't like the thought of you staying here even one night with that man lurking."

Grace sat down at the quilting frame and picked up a needle, drawing a kerosene lamp closer on an adjacent table and balancing her crutches against the wall. She drew the light blue thread through the chambray inner square of the quilt and Seth frowned.

"What are you doing?"

"Quilting."

"I know that. I mean, shouldn't you head to bed to get some rest for tomorrow?"

Grace nodded. "I will, but I've several hours of work left on this. It's due to send out to Lancaster first thing in the morning. I can get it done before the wedding."

Seth knew that she made her living by quilting. He watched her small hands work diligently at the cloth, her slender neck bent. He didn't want her to be working when she should have a chance to rest. And it didn't help that she seemed to have completely forgotten him as she picked up her stitches.

"Lancaster can wait for the quilt. We're going to be married."

She looked up at him, her eyes earnest. "*Ach*, but this is a special order. A wedding anniversary quilt. A remake of a Double Nine-Patch Chain with cotton percale and sateen as well as the chambray. I can't stop yet."

Her voice ended on a faintly pleading note, and he felt a surge of remorse for being critical. He knew what it was like to be close to finishing a painting and then to have to stop.

He grabbed a chair, straddled it, and sat down. Then he reached across the expanse of fabric and slid a needle from the quilt roll.

"What are you doing?"

He grinned at her. "Quilting."

"No, you're not."

He threaded the needle with an easy hand and bent to begin to stitch.

"*Ach*, please don't. You'll ruin . . ." Her voice trailed away, and Seth looked up after he'd completed five perfect stitches.

Grace stared at him like he had two heads. "Wherever did you learn?"

"I worked on Lilly's wedding quilt a bit and I picked it up, that's all. I kind of think of it as painting, but with fabric."

Grace smiled at him, but he had the strange feeling that the smile was a veil, something between them but not meant to draw them together. "The bishop might have an admonition for you for speaking of painting and quilting in such a manner. You make it sound like art."

Seth paused in mid-stitch. He had no idea how she'd respond if she knew about the painting that he did in secret. He opted for a cautious approach with Grace, though he hardly knew how he'd keep it from her once she'd seen his bedroom.

"You don't like art?"

"We are not permitted." Her shrug was dismissive, but he felt the instinct to pursue.

"Was the last *Amisch* community you lived in very conservative?"

"Very."

"Perhaps you will find some things different here."

"I—I already do, of course." She seemed to be searching for a comfortable footing in their talk, and it puzzled him.

"Then how do you personally feel about art?"

She stopped stitching to look up at him. "I—I have not considered . . ."

He nodded. "Our people usually don't. But you surely understand art and beauty, considering your quilt creations here."

"'There is no beauty without purpose.'" She quoted the old Amish adage as if she'd caught hold of a lifeline.

He wouldn't press any further—upsetting his bride was not good form. He bowed his head, then grinned at her.

"I yield to the proverb."

Grace watched his golden head catch the light of the lamp as he worked, and she resumed her quilting with a tangled sense of relief and curiosity. In truth, she saw art in the simplest of things: a spider's web glittered with dew, the bend of Abel's neck, the flowing mane of a horse. But Silas had taught her a dark silence of the soul and mind. He had compressed her sense of self until there was nothing left. Seth Wyse, however, seemed altogether different. In a way, that frightened her more than any of Silas's punishments. For she could not give him something that was gone—the girl she once had been.

And the woman she was now seemed like a poor substitute.

CHAPTER 9

"Where have you been? It's past three a.m." Jacob said irritably.

Seth's shoulders drooped with fatigue. All he wanted was the refuge of his bed for a brief hour. He blinked in the inky darkness and then a lamp flickered. Jacob lay sprawled in his bed.

"Lilly throw you out?" Seth asked as he started to undress.

"Funny, *bruder*. *Nee*, I told you I'd help you, and I have a promise to keep." Jacob tossed a rolled quilt at him and he caught it with weariness.

"What's this?"

"Tabitha King's Bachelor's Choice quilt, remember? She's invited to the wedding, by the way."

Seth groaned, putting the quilt on a dresser as he slid off his shirt. "Why is she invited? The woman is crazy as a loon."

"Don't you remember? The quilt is her gift to you, so that when you sleep under it, you'll dream of your future bride."

"I don't have time to sleep, let alone dream. And I happen to know my future bride. Now, get out of my bed."

Jacob hefted himself up. "Want me to tuck you in?"

"Go away."

Seth dropped onto the mattress with a sigh of pleasure. He felt it when Jacob slid the quilt over him but was too tired to care as sleep engulfed him.

Her black hair was short. It bothered him because it seemed all wrong for an Amish woman, but when he ran his hands through the silky curls, he felt his heart turn over. Her back was to him and he bent to snuggle closer to her petite frame. She smelled of fresh linen and sunshine. He threaded his fingers around her belly, and she rubbed tenderly at the blue paint stains that smudged his hands.

Then something intervened—a sinister black shadow that seemed to arise from the ground between them, pushing him away and engulfing her. He tried to break through, called her name, then called it again, frantic: "Grace!"

"Seth, do you have to be hollering your bride's name out loud even on your wedding morning?"

His mother stood over his bed, a smile on her lips as she lifted the edge of the Bachelor's Choice quilt. "I guess Tabitha King was right."

Seth levered himself up on one elbow and blinked sleepily in the light of the new dawn. The quilt slipped from his shoulder, and he reached to feel the colorful fabric. He had dreamed of his bride, but it had been disturbing rather than pleasant. What had Jacob said about Grace? Deep water. Perhaps he should pray for stamina to swim.

He grinned wryly to himself, then reached an arm up to catch his mom around the waist, pulling her with ease onto the edge of the bed and giving her a quick hug.

She giggled like a girl. "*Ach*, Seth . . ."

"Has anyone told you lately how *wunderbaar* a *mamm* you are?"

"A gentleman might tell me," she said primly.

"Well, gentleman or not, this man will tell you that it takes a special mother to welcome a new daughter-in-law and grandson on a day's notice, and my bet is that you have been up for quite a while baking and such."

"I did hear you come in late. Would you forgive a special mother for asking what you were doing at that hour?"

He smiled at her tenderly. "Quilting, *Mamm*. Quilting."

"All right. I'll try to believe that if you'll allow me one more question."

He settled back on the bed and folded his arms behind his head. "Anything."

"Seth, forgive me, but I—we—your *fater* and I would have to be blind not to notice the way you've felt about Grace right along. But she didn't seem to return the favor. I just wonder if, perhaps, the two of you made a mistake somewhere along the line. Both women and men can do that, you know. It's just that—well, if I'm to be a grandmother again soon, I'd rather hear it from your lips first than, say, Esther Zook's . . ."

She trailed off helplessly, blushing.

Seth laughed out loud. "Mother, are you asking me if Grace is pregnant?"

"*Jah*, I'm sorry."

"Don't be sorry. I know it all seems wild, but no, Grace is not carrying my child."

She patted his cheek with a sigh. "That's all right then. I mean, it would have been all right the other way—not that it would have been right, you realize. But . . . I mean—"

Seth laughed again. "*Mamm*, you are a treasure."

"What are you doing, *Mamm*?"

Grace turned from the trunk where she balanced unevenly on one leg and the walking cast. "You're up early, even for your birthday."

"What are you doing?" he repeated.

"Looking for a dress to wear to the wedding. Happy birthday."

"What dress did you wear then?"

"Then?" Grace tried to catch him close for a hug, but he allowed it for only a moment.

"Then—when you married *Fater*."

Grace drew a steadying breath. What had she worn? It was all a nightmarish blur . . . Blue. Of course it would have been blue.

"Then? It was a blue dress, I think. I guess I'll wear this one today. It's more purple."

Abel spun slowly around, his toe in a groove on the floor. "But you always wear black."

Grace shut her eyes against the memory. It was true. Silas had drained all of the color out of her life, including in what she was permitted to wear. She fingered the fabric in her hand and swallowed the lump in her throat. Would Seth Wyse care what she wore? It didn't matter. Clothes were nothing to her anymore.

She looped the dress over one arm, then limped to the kitchen to eat the breakfast that Violet had prepared.

CHAPTER 10

Tobias Beiler had taken great pains with his appearance and brushed into the Wyse home with a smile and a nod to the small woman greeting people at the door.

"Uh, forgive me—I'm Seth's mother, Mary Wyse. Are you a close relative?"

"Indeed I am." He smiled faintly. "Of the bride."

Mary Wyse nodded, her hazel eyes puzzled. "Then come in, please. Grace is upstairs getting ready, but my son is here, and Abel."

"*Danki*. I'll make myself at home." He moved past her as more people entered, then scanned the crowd. His eyes suddenly locked on his nephew's, and he saw the child tremble with fear. He grinned and strolled over.

"Hello, hero. Hiya, Abel. I've come to wish you well. Both you and your sweet *mamm*, of course." He put a hand on the boy's shaking shoulder and Seth knocked it off with a casual move.

"What are you doing here?"

"It's my right to see this wedding performed, to

assure that it's not some sham to protect a beautiful woman," Tobias said. Seth stared at him, and he felt the sudden tingle of fear.

"Abel, go and stand with Jacob for a while. It's all right. I will speak to your—this man," Seth said.

Tobias lifted a glass of water from a nearby table and eyed Seth over the rim as Abel wandered off. "Are you sure she's worth being saddled with him? Looks through your soul, he does."

Tobias saw the tension in the younger man's body and went on softly. "So, Seth, is it? What do you think your wedding night's going to be like, after all those years with my brother?"

"You have five seconds before I rip your throat out right here."

Tobias laughed out loud, then realized he was attracting attention. A tall, dark haired-man with flashing eyes crossed the room.

"Trouble here, little *bruder*?" the man asked.

"Nothing I can't work out."

"*Jah*, but you shouldn't have to work anything out—not on your wedding day. Allow me."

Tobias struggled against the man's iron grip. "I have a right to be here. Tell him, hero."

Seth gave a curt nod, and the dark-haired man relaxed his grip a little. "Not one word," he breathed. "You stay at the back of the room, and when this is over, you're gone. Get it?"

Tobias gritted his teeth at the bone-crunching pain in his arm and nodded. "*Jah*."

Seth watched Jacob escort Tobias Beiler across the room with what appeared to be a casual air, but he knew the strength in his brother's hand. Beiler was practically wincing by the time they reached an obscure corner.

Seth drew a deep, shaky breath. He'd never lost his temper so badly, but for a brief moment, he thought he might lay hands on Beiler. Thanks be to *Gott*, Jacob had intervened.

Seth looked around, found Abel frozen among a small swirl of guests, and went to him. He stooped down and fooled with the child's pant cuff, not wanting anyone to listen. "Abel, it's all right. Do you hear me?"

"Mama said the bad man would go away if we married you."

"He will," Seth said. "As soon as your mama and I are married. As soon as me and you are married, right? Jacob's got the bad man and won't let him go. You're safe."

The boy's lower lip trembled. "I want my *mamm*."

"She's upstairs. She doesn't know the bad man's here. Let's keep it a secret between us men? Then she won't worry, then she'll be happy. She's safe, Abel. I promise."

Seth waited with some anxiety while the child thought. Grace would be terrified to know Beiler was there. He didn't want that to color the beginning of their life together. Besides, Jacob would handle it.

"All right," Abel agreed. "Between us men."

Seth dragged his attention back to the boy. "Brave man. Stand by me while we get ready for your *mamm* to walk in, all right? And don't worry. Everything's going to be fine."

Grace had accepted Mary Wyse's offer of help and now found herself upstairs with Jacob's wife, Lilly, sitting in light underthings while Lilly pressed her purple dress. She could have managed, she supposed—she always had before—but still it was nice to have the help. Grace had arranged her own hair and *kapp* at home, and Seth had brought her over and helped her upstairs. Violet had disappeared shortly after they arrived, probably helping Mary Wyse with the preparations downstairs.

Grace glanced at Lilly—tall, dark-haired, and elegant in her simplicity. She was the local schoolteacher, and Abel adored her.

"Seth told me that you're expecting," Grace said shyly.

Lilly looked up from the heavy iron and smiled. "*Jah*, we are. We're so happy."

Grace nodded in understanding. "Pregnancy can be a special time between a couple, I would imagine."

Lilly brought the warm dress to her. "I'm sorry that you have to imagine such a thing. Did you not—I mean, was your first husband not affectionate?"

Grace shook her head. "*Nee*, he was not."

"Well, Seth will be," Lilly said stoutly. "And he'll be an excellent father to Abel and all the *kinner* that come along."

Grace knew she should feel reassured, but the idea of carrying Seth's baby terrified her. She wondered if she would ever be able to trust him like a wife should.

She slipped on the dress and allowed Lilly to fuss with the folds. Her gaze drifted to the small bureau mirror, where she caught a glimpse of her own eyes. Purple pools of sadness in a wan face.

Not the eyes of a happy woman.

Not the face of a bride.

Violet skimmed a finger down the length of the flower's stem and covertly eyed the man who was spending a lot of time tending to his horses. He wasn't handsome in any conventional sense of the word, but there was something about him. Something . . . interesting. Mary Wyse had asked her to run outside and pick a few flowers for the table, and here she was dawdling, waylaid by her own thoughts.

She grabbed a few more flowers and then stepped behind a bush so she wouldn't be seen spying on him. What was he doing? He had pulled something from his horse's side and held it cupped in his hand. He bent over it for a moment, then straightened up and came straight toward her.

She ducked down as he approached the bush and deposited a green baby caterpillar on a large leaf. Then, just when she thought she was safe, he looked through the branches and saw her.

He flushed, visibly startled.

She shielded her eyes to blink up at him in the summer's sun. "Hello. Are you here for Seth? I'm Violet Raber, the bride's sister. I'm supposed to help greet the guests." She glanced at the inching caterpillar. "And that was very nice."

The man's hazel eyes narrowed as he gazed down at

her with a frown. "Then shouldn't you be inside?" he asked.

Violet was undaunted. "I'm to greet the guests—you included, apparently."

"Luke King," he said tersely.

"*Ach* . . . may I call you Luke?" she asked, lifting the flowers to her nose in a coy gesture and stepping from behind the leaves.

"*Nee,*" he snapped, then brushed past her to mount the steps of the house.

The thought dropped into her mind fully formed, and yet instinctively she knew it was true. There was something about him, something she couldn't quite put her finger on. Something she liked.

She found herself humming as she finished gathering the flowers. "Now that," she murmured to herself, "is a man worth pursuing."

CHAPTER 11

"A woman is like a wrapped gift . . ."

Bishop Loftus paused, and Seth resisted the urge to laugh. The sacred vows had already been said, and now the bishop had begun to give the traditional admonitions and exhortations. But Bishop Loftus wasn't exactly traditional in his approaches, and there was simply no way to predict what the good man might say. He had an odd way of making his point.

"*Jah*, a wrapped gift," the old man went on. "And if she will open herself to her community, her children, her husband, then she will be a continual source of blessing. But this gift needs to be handled with care—sacred care."

Seth felt his mind begin to drift as the bishop droned on. He thought with pleasure of how *gut* Abel looked after he and Jacob had suited him up. He loved the way Grace's eyes had shone with something like happiness when she'd seen her son, but there had also been a soberness about her. Seth gazed down at his bride as she stood across from him, and then Beiler's sinister words seeped through his mind like dark oil.

"Do you so promise, Seth Wyse?" The bishop's voice snapped him back to the moment and he stared at the man, feeling his face flush as the keen, knowing old eyes swept over him.

"I—uh, of course. Of course I promise." There was a general rustling and sigh of approval from the few family and friends seated behind them, and Seth slowly exhaled with relief, having absolutely no idea what he'd committed to.

"*Gut!*" The bishop nodded with approval and a wry smile. "And, Grace, will you do the same?"

"*Jah.*"

Her soft reply sent an odd tingling down Seth's spine and he shifted his weight.

Then there was a brief concluding prayer, and he turned with Grace to face the small gathering. Seth saw Jacob escorting Beiler out the back screen door and exhaled a sigh of relief and satisfaction. He had kept Grace and Abel safe.

Yet it was *der Herr,* his conscience reminded him, who had truly arranged things. He said a silent prayer of thanks, and then they were engulfed in the goodwill of those present.

Violet watched as Grant and Sarah Williams went to congratulate Grace and Seth, accompanied by Sarah's brother, the enigmatic Luke King.

Grace and Violet were distant cousins of the King family, and Sarah Williams was formerly a King, so although they barely knew each other, there was a very distant family connection.

Violet had gone to some trouble to have introductions properly made between her and her King relatives, including Luke. Then she went about the room, ferreting out every last piece of information that she could about Sarah and her family. Her husband, Grant, had been an *Englisch* veterinarian who moved to the community two years prior. Grant had fallen in love with Sarah and converted to be Amish.

And Luke? Twenty-three. Sworn bachelor. Farmer. Married to his work.

Violet smiled to herself. *He doesn't stand a chance.*

Tobias Beiler yanked at his stiff shirt collar and drove the distance to Fibber's Motel, outside of Lockport. The place was not to his liking, with its lime-green paint and flashing neon sign, but it was somewhere no Amish would ever come looking for him.

He entered his room and crushed a cockroach with a heavy boot, then made for the bed. There he picked up his Bible and began to read from Genesis. He liked the story of when Abram, later Abraham, gave the first choice over the best of the land to his nephew and Lot took it.

Tobias smiled. This no doubt hasty marriage of Grace's was but a temporary setback until *Gott* gave him the choice of things most pleasant in life.

He picked up his heavy, leather-bound journal and a pen and flipped through the unlined pages to mark the date. *My dear departed brother,* he wrote, *I toast you with wedding water. Grace is married, literally at the eleventh hour, but I am not yet vanquished. I will have her, and all that is rightfully mine . . .*

CHAPTER 12

Grace caught Abel against her hip and watched with cautious pleasure as Seth bent to whisper in her son's ear. It must have been a good secret, because a rare smile crossed the boy's face. Seth straightened up and reached to hold her hand.

She was unused to such casual tenderness and touch. Over the years she had grown accustomed to Silas's bruising grip, and she wondered what it would be like to truly relax into the calloused strength of Seth's hand.

Her husband's hand.

She smiled as Lilly and Jacob approached. They did indeed look like a couple expecting their first child as they touched shoulders and smiled. Grace wondered if she would ever look at her new husband with that much love.

"Grace, you look so beautiful, as always," Lilly said gaily.

Although Grace nodded her thanks, a knot of anxiety twisted inside her at the words. She should have been pleased with the compliment. But she had learned from Silas that beauty was a curse, not a gift.

"And, Abel, a happy birthday to you!" Lilly went on. "Jacob and I have a special present for you later."

Grace prodded her son gently, and he murmured his thanks.

Seth's mother came to lead them to the head seats at the kitchen table. There was no formal *eck* or bridal table, as there would have been for a first-time bride, but leaves had been added to accommodate the guests; and Grace appreciated all the effort Seth's mother had gone to. The table was laden with ham, mashed potatoes, green beans, steaming gravy, cooked celery, and two huge frosted cakes, one with the fluffy white boiled icing Abel loved so much. She was grateful to her new family for acknowledging her son's birthday.

They all bowed for a moment of silent thanks, and Grace prayed that she might be a good wife to the younger man next to her. It occurred to her that she had no idea how old he was. She'd have to ask.

She almost jumped when she felt him lean in next to her ear. "Prayer's over, sweetheart. Can you pass the potatoes?"

Grace looked up with a flush of embarrassment. All eyes were on her, and Seth's hand gently enfolded hers. She broke free of his grasp to lift the heavy bowl of potatoes, and then the moment passed and the guests began to laugh and talk and eat.

Grace glanced over at Abel, seated securely between Jacob and Samuel Wyse, and saw with relief that he was heartily eating the food piled in front of him.

"I think he's having a *gut* time," Seth said.

Grace turned to look at him, not prepared for the intensity in his blue eyes. She nodded briefly in agreement and toyed with her food.

"You don't want to be told that you're beautiful, do you?" he asked under cover of the general talk. Grace felt a lump begin to grow in her throat.

"How . . . how do you know?" she whispered.

"Because when Lilly said it, you sort of tensed up. But I'd like to say it."

"Well, don't," she said. She felt a catch of dismay and looked at him, expecting a rebuke. But he continued to smile at her, poised and patient.

"Grace Wyse, I think you'll find that you can say just about anything and you won't rile me. And I'll try not to rile you, my . . . *fraa*."

He didn't say the word *beautiful*, but its implication hung in the air, laden with promise, a promise requested by the bishop that Grace knew she would have to struggle to keep.

"So is it a waste of time to ask if you have any questions about the wedding night?"

Jacob spoke in the summer twilight air and Seth shot him a sour look. "Nice, Jacob. Thanks, but *nee*. Besides, you and Lilly—I mean, well, I know there were some problems."

Jacob smiled. "It was worth the wait. But my wedding night? Well, let's just say that after a few days I started sleeping on the floor."

Seth shrugged. "Maybe that's where I should start."

"Two people can sleep in a bed, Seth, and just *sleep*. Maybe you should put a bundling board between you."

They both laughed at the reference to the old custom

of putting a board between an engaged couple and letting them share a bed. Then Jacob grew serious.

"Seth, that man, Grace's former brother-in-law—there's something not right there. I don't think he's going to let go as easily as he did today. I want you to be careful."

Seth nodded. "I've thought of it. I'll watch."

"Then watch well. I don't want to be an only child."

Seth frowned. "You don't think he's as bad as all that, do you?"

Jacob thought for a moment, then drew a deep breath. "There have been times, when I've gone to buy a maimed or beaten horse from a cruel buyer—there's a look in that person's eyes. It's almost as if they have to tell themselves that there'll be another horse to abuse and they can let this one go. But there's only one you, one Grace, one Abel. I think Tobias Beiler is capable of anything."

Seth nodded. "I see Lilly coming. I'd better head back in."

Jacob caught him by the sleeve, then gave him a rough hug. "Keep your chin up, *bruder.*"

"Right."

"Hey, I almost forgot—your wedding present, and Abel's birthday present." Jacob turned him in the direction of one of the smaller barns as Lilly joined them.

"Should I get Grace?" Seth asked.

"I think you should be the one to give this to Grace and Abel," Lilly replied, running ahead a bit to slide the barn door open.

Seth expected a colt. He knew some of the mares from their horse-breeding farm were about ready to foal, but Lilly led them instead to a small pen as Jacob lit a kerosene lamp.

Lilly stooped down, then lifted a small, soft puppy up into her arms. A golden retriever, by the looks of her fur and the shape of her head. "Isn't she *wunderbaar*?"

Seth smiled with real pleasure.

"I read an article that said dogs can sometimes help children like Abel to feel more calm and comfortable," Lilly said, handing him the puppy.

"That's great. *Danki*, both of you. It's a perfect present to start wedded life."

Seth cuddled the small body against him and thought with pleasure of giving it to his new family.

Family. The word echoed in his mind. He could hardly believe that he was married to the woman he'd longed for over the past months. Tomorrow he would ask Grace about adopting Abel so the boy could share his name, if he wanted.

The puppy stretched to lick his chin and Jacob laughed. "Looks like another girl is smitten by your charm, *bruder.*"

"*Jah,*" Lilly added. "A charm you're going to have to apply only to your wife now."

"That will be no problem," Seth said. "No problem at all."

CHAPTER 13

Grace had tried to help with the *redding-up* but was hastily shooed away by a flurry of ladies. So she hobbled into the living room and propped up on the couch. Abel soon joined her and she lightly stroked his dark hair until he fell asleep by her side.

Tired. So tired. She closed her eyes and drifted, and her mind carried her back to the early morning of this long, long day.

She had put the finishing touches on the quilt just before nine a.m. Seth came by to drive her to the post office to get it out in time.

The postmistress, Edith, had obviously heard through the grapevine of their wedding and teased Grace lightly as she paid for her parcel. "Probably won't have to keep your quilting business going now, will you, honey? This boy's as rich as can be."

"*Ach*, I don't know. I—"

"Now, Edith," Seth said, "Grace can quilt all she likes or doesn't like. It'll be up to her. And don't go spouting off about money when I know what a little nest egg you've got going."

Edith straightened her *kapp* and winked at them. "Might go to Vegas someday."

"With the bishop?" Seth asked, and they all laughed.

Then Edith produced a letter for Grace. "It's from Middle Hollow, Ohio. Used to live there, right?"

"*Jah.*" Grace took the letter with trepidation, fearing it might be some legal paper from Tobias Beiler.

"What is it?" Seth had asked urgently, bending over her shoulder with concern.

"It's all right. It's from a friend." She cut a glance at Edith. "I'll read it later."

With Seth close behind, Grace made her exit, leaving Edith disappointed and crestfallen.

Grace rubbed her eyes and slid the unopened letter out of her apron pocket. It was from Alice Miller, her only real friend in Middle Hollow. Alice was *Englisch*, and Silas had hired her to help cook and clean when Grace was pregnant and sick in the early months of carrying Abel.

Alice had become a lifeline for Grace—the only person who saw through the religious façade Silas wore, the only one who so much as suspected the abuse. The only one who knew where Grace was going when she fled Middle Hollow after her husband's death.

Repeatedly Alice had urged Grace to leave Silas, and repeatedly Grace had refused. What Alice didn't know—couldn't know—was how far Silas was willing to go to keep her under his control. Grace had to protect Abel. She could not take the chance of losing him or being separated from him.

Grace scanned the letter and her heart sank. Alice's

husband, Bud, had passed away. Alice asked if there was any way she might come and visit for a spell. She needed to get away, she said. Just for a while.

Grace knew how much Alice and Bud loved each other. How she must be grieving.

But what would Seth say to their having company so soon after they had married—especially since Violet was with them? Still, Alice would be no trouble . . .

She'd talk to Seth about it. Soon.

Right after she closed her eyes for just a few minutes . . .

She thought she might be dreaming but didn't seem to care enough to wake, she felt so fuzzily warm and pleasant. She cuddled closer to Abel, then jerked awake to find herself pressed against Seth's chest with her hand on his. She moved to draw away, and he let her go easily.

"You must be exhausted," he said. "But I think you might have enough energy to enjoy at least one wedding gift." He pointed to the floor, where Abel was lolling about with a reddish-gold puppy.

"*Mamm*, look! Her name's Pretty. I named her. Is that okay?"

Grace eased upward on the couch. The guests were all gone. She must have been asleep for quite some time.

"Of course." She smiled. She glanced at Seth. "Seems a dog might be good for him. My husband—that is, my former husband—"

"Wouldn't allow it," Seth finished. "Yes, so you've told me."

He leaned his broad back against the cushions, moving a bit closer. She forced herself to sit still, to resist the desire to flee from such intimate touch. She didn't know how to handle his gentleness and prayed that it was no ploy. Yet she trusted him with Abel and the horses; surely she could learn to trust him herself.

"It seems that there was much your husband wouldn't allow." It was more statement than question. She murmured an affirmation under cover of Abel's laughter. A rare sound, and a delightful one.

"Well, this husband is different."

He smiled at her, and for a moment she felt herself cast back into that girlhood fantasy—the handsome *Amisch* boy with golden hair and perfectly chiseled features.

But things were not always what they seemed.

Least of all a person's heart.

"*Sohn*, your *mamm* and I are going to move out to the *daudi haus* tonight. We've got the bedroom here all fixed so you and Grace can have it. I wanted to let you know."

Seth raised his eyebrows at his father across the back of Star Bright. "What?"

It was the custom of their people that parents would often move out of the main house to a smaller adjacent residence, but Seth hadn't thought that far. He tried to imagine him and Grace and Abel rambling around in that huge three-story farmhouse.

"I talked to Jacob," his father went on. "He's bent

on building up the farm that he and Lilly are in with her *mamm*."

Seth sighed inwardly. Jacob was content living with Lilly and her mother. Lilly's *mamm* had battled depression for quite some time but was growing better every day. Still, the fact remained that his *bruder* had every right to this home. And even though Lilly's family's sprawling white farmhouse was large enough, it was no comparison to the Wyse home.

"*Daed*, I can't let you. I feel like I'm uprooting you and *Mamm*. Grace and I can manage with the *daudi haus* and then move when . . . well, if—"

His father laughed. "When more *grandkinner* come along, eh? Well, that probably won't be long. We're getting a head start, that's all. It's the way of things, Seth. You know that."

Seth nodded. His *daed* was right. It was the way of things.

He only wondered exactly how he was going to navigate Grace to the master bedroom without appearing overly eager.

CHAPTER 14

Tobias Beiler left the run-down motel room and retrieved his horse and buggy from the old garage out back, then drove to the end of town and stopped at a restaurant called Pinky's. There Amish buggies were tied to a hitching post among *Englisch* cars. It was just the kind of place where he might find the information he needed.

He went inside, pulling his hat low in case any of the wedding guests were present.

He needn't have worried. Nobody in the place looked even vaguely familiar. He slid into a back booth, facing away from the door. A tall, thin *Englischer* approached him with a menu. "You new around here?" the man asked.

Tobias nodded and handed back the menu. "Burger. Rare."

"How about a shake? We make 'em nice and thick."

Tobias swallowed. Milk products upset his stomach, but being agreeable seemed more important. "Sure. Chocolate."

"Got it. Anything else?"

"I might be looking for work, if you know anybody who's hiring," Tobias said.

The *Englischer* scratched his chin. "Try Deacon Zook, just east of town," he said. "His hired man just moved on, so he might be wanting somebody."

"Thanks for the tip," Tobias said. "For an *Englischer*, you know a lot about what goes on around here."

The man grinned. "See that sign on the window? Pinky's?"

Tobias nodded.

"Well, I'm Pinky. I've been here for years. You need something, just ask."

"But I want to sleep with you." Abel's voice rose a fraction, and Grace hastened to soothe him before anyone could hear. She'd gotten into the habit of letting him crawl into her bed late at night or early in the morning, a luxury she could never have afforded with Silas. And now, Abel was understandably upset at the prospect of sleeping in his own room in a strange house.

Not that she wasn't a bit concerned about similar things herself. She knew Seth was a gentleman, but—

"Mamm!"

"What's the trouble here?" Seth stood in the doorway of the kitchen, smiling. He'd changed into a blue work shirt to do chores, and his face was pleasantly flushed.

"It's nothing," Grace hurried to assure him.

"Jah, it be," Abel bawled out.

"Abel, please be quiet. Think of Seth's parents," Grace said tightly.

Seth waved a hand. *"Nee*, don't worry. My parents

have tucked themselves up in the *daudi haus*, starting tonight."

"Well there," Abel cried. "Then there's lots of room. Please, *Mamm*?"

Grace met Seth's eyes in apology. "He's afraid of a new house and wants to stay with me, but I've told him—"

"He can come in with us." Seth shrugged. "It's a big bed."

Abel suddenly raced across the room and began to beat at Seth with small fists. "No, no, no! You'll not make *Mamm* sleep with you and make her cry in the night like *Fater* used to! I won't let you. I won't let you!"

Pretty's shrill barks added to the chaos. "Whoa, whoa there, buddy. I don't want to make your *mamm* cry, not a drop." Grace could see that Seth was gently holding the boy off, but he was visibly confused. He looked over Abel's head to Grace.

"Abel, *sei so gut*. I've told you Seth is not like—" She broke off.

Grace watched as a tense awareness entered Seth's features. He dropped to his knees in front of the struggling child and began to speak in a soft voice that somehow soothed her as well.

"Abel, listen to me. I will never hurt your mother, at least never on purpose. You can trust me. Have you ever seen me hurt the horses when I take you riding?"

Abel had stopped his violent movements to slouch on the floor near the dog. "*Nee*. You think *Mamm's* like a horse?"

"Beautiful and free like a horse, *jah*. But she's a bit prettier in the face."

Grace held her breath, waiting. Then Abel smiled, getting the joke.

"You're silly, Seth."

Seth nodded, then reached out to brush her son's dark hair with a gentle finger. "Yeah, I guess I am."

Seth listened to the even breathing of the child who lay between them. It was dark now, so he could let go of the tears he'd been holding back. They seeped down his cheeks and pooled at the back of his neck.

It was his wedding night, and here he was crying like a babe, but he couldn't help himself. He thought of what Abel had screamed—that Grace had been made to cry in the night. It tore at him, and he longed to reach through the ice of the past to strangle Silas Beiler.

"Are you asleep?" It was Grace's voice, disembodied, drifting to him in the darkness.

"*Nee*," he choked out, swiping hastily at his face in the dark.

"Why are you crying?"

He almost smiled. How perceptive she was. But perhaps that perception was born out of necessity, to keep herself guarded and safe. It didn't bear thinking about.

"For you," he whispered.

"Well, don't." He heard the crisp sheets rustle as if she'd swatted at them in disgust. "I tried to tell you that I'm not what I appear to be, will never fit your imaginings. Nor will I ever be able to fully keep the promise I made to you as part of our wedding."

He swallowed. The promise. Why couldn't he remember?

"It doesn't matter," he said.

"Of course it matters. And it seems strange to me that you're willing to settle for . . . damaged goods."

He forced himself to absorb the pain her words brought, and the anger. "We are what we are in this moment, Grace Wyse. The past is gone. Don't think of yourself like that."

She laughed mirthlessly. "Do you really believe that? Of course, you probably do. You've lived such a charmed life that you can easily dismiss what's past."

He heard her draw a deep breath as if she was surprised at what she'd said, then her voice came softer. "I—I'm so sorry. *Sei so gut*, forgive me. I—I'm not like this."

He heard her move and realized she'd laid a protective arm across Abel's body. Seth turned on his side, facing them. He reached out a hand and touched her arm in the dark. Her skin was so soft, like the petals of a damp rose. He trailed his fingers down to the fine bones of her fingers and let his hand rest there. "I meant what I told Abel—I won't hurt you or him—ever."

Her hand shook under his, and then she slid away. "Yes, you will," she whispered so faintly that he thought perhaps he'd imagined it. "Yes, you will."

CHAPTER 15

Grace was up as the first light of dawn came through the large window and fell across her husband's face. Already a bit of reddish-blond shadow darkened the line of his jaw and the cleft in his chin. The sunlight played on his thick lashes, lying heavy against his cheekbones, and brought out the rich tones of his golden hair. He looked so beautiful and so very young. Grace felt old next to him, old and frightened of the emotions that churned within her.

She played with the *kapp* strings that brushed her cheek, glad he hadn't mentioned it when she'd worn it to bed out of habit.

Her gaze trailed down the line of his neck to the breadth of his bare shoulders and chest, and then she realized that Abel was snuggled up next to him—Abel and his puppy. Boy and dog were pillowed on one muscular arm, forcing Seth into an awkward position with a tangle of sheets about his waist and long legs. She looked down at the strong hand that lay palm up on the bed so very near her. His fingers were relaxed, curled inward, and she saw that he had neat fingernails, marred only by some faint smudges of yellow and blue paint.

She puzzled over the paint. What had he been doing with such colors around the farm?

"I paint," he said hoarsely.

She flinched as if she'd been caught spying on him, then she met his eyes.

"What?"

"I paint. Paintings."

"Why?" Her whisper was shocked, and the smile deepened in his sleepy, heated gaze.

He eased his arm a bit from beneath Abel, and the child stirred but did not waken. Pretty regarded them with sober brown eyes, then stretched, sighed, and went back to sleep.

"For fun. For release," he whispered back. "Don't you ever quilt for that reason?"

"*Nee*. It's vanity," Grace said. A shock ran through her like ice water in her veins when she realized that she was parroting Silas. "I guess . . . ," she added lamely.

"You guess?"

"Does the bishop know?"

He laughed softly, a flash of even white teeth. "*Nee*, you've got me there, but I'd like to invite you to visit my old bedroom sometime. It's where I paint, though I guess the light would probably be better up in one of the attics."

"I—I'd like to visit."

"*Gut*," he answered as Abel began to stir. "Really *gut*."

Grace felt as if she'd committed to an intimacy somehow. She cleared her throat. "Seth, I—well, there's something I want to ask. It's okay if you say no—"

He laughed quietly. "Give me a chance, Grace. What do you need?"

"That letter from Edith, at the post office. I told you it was from a friend?"

He nodded, and she went on in a rush. "Well, it was from an *Englisch* woman named Alice Miller. She truly loved her husband, and he recently passed on. She wondered if she might come and visit for a while. To get away. Of course, there's no way for her to know I'm married now . . ."

After a long moment, he shrugged a bare shoulder. "All right. Ask her to come, but on one condition."

"What?" Grace asked, suddenly wary of the deepened tone of his voice.

"I'll agree to Alice Miller coming if you agree to try to relax and have some fun with me once in a while." He gave her a steady look.

She nodded her head in agreement, then watched as Abel awoke to smile and tickle Pretty.

CHAPTER 16

Alice Miller climbed gamely into the blue van driven by a local teenager. He was glad of the money and said he didn't mind making the trip so long as he could listen to his music. Besides, he'd made the drive not long before and knew the way.

Alice sighed at the confusion of loud drums and guitar strains coming from the radio. It was going to be a long trip, but one she needed to make. Since Bud had passed, she was terrified of staying alone in the small house. She knew her fears were irrational, and she'd even thought about taking the medication her doctor prescribed to help calm her down.

But after much prayer, she had felt led to write to Grace and go and visit instead. Muttering a vain wish for ear plugs, she settled her Pink Lady sales cosmetic bag against the door speaker, trying to absorb the din. She glanced into the visor mirror once and saw a tired face, gray hair, and a ridiculously bright hair band she'd put on early that morning in an effort to be cheerful. Bud had loved color . . .

"It looks dumb," she muttered aloud.

"What's that, Miss Alice?" Tommy yelled.

Alice shook her head and closed her eyes.

Seth hadn't slept well with Abel and the puppy piled on top of him, and he had the circles beneath his eyes to prove it. Jacob must have noticed because he caught Seth's arm as they entered the barn.

"What?" Seth asked, shaking him off.

"Tougher night than you thought?"

"Why?"

"You've got bruises under your eyes for want of sleep."

"I'm newly married, remember? There are bound to be some changes." Seth turned a shoulder on his brother and went to grab a bridle off the wall.

"Do you really think you can hide anything from me, little *bruder*?"

"There's nothing to hide."

"So everything is perfect?"

"Right as rain." Seth moved toward a stall, but Jacob stepped in front of him, arms crossed.

"Seth, come on."

"Move, Jacob, or I'll knock you flat."

"Will you? Over genuine worry?"

Seth sighed aloud, then let his shoulders drop. He was too tired to argue and, in truth, he longed to talk with his brother. "You were right, okay? Grace is deep water, and I find that I don't swim so well against the current."

He set the bridle down and dropped onto a hay bale, leaning back against a beam. Jacob moved to sit opposite him. "You've had words with her already?"

"*Nee*, of course not. That's the funny thing, though. She'll spark up at me for something or another, and then she'll back off or wait, as if—well, as if I'm going to do something to her."

"Do something to her?"

Seth dropped his head and covered his face with his hands. "Her first husband—she hasn't come right out and said this, but I think he hurt her. Physically, I mean."

"What?"

Seth swiped at his eyes and looked at his brother. "I want to kill him. I know it's stupid—the man's dead, but he's still there somehow, between us. She won't let me come close and I can't fault her. I mean, who would ever trust another man after—well, after that?"

"She knows you're a different man."

"Does she? How? Abel's eight, so she must have been married for at least close to nine years. How long was it before this Silas Beiler started to do whatever he did? Maybe he seemed okay at first."

Jacob shook his head. "Why don't you come right out and ask her? It might bring you closer."

"Or drive us further apart."

"Have you prayed about it?"

"*Jah*. A little." Seth squeezed his eyes shut tight for a moment. "I could pray more."

"I'll pray for you," Jacob promised.

"*Danki*, big *bruder*."

"Why don't you take a walk before work today? Kiss your wife *gut* morning?"

"I wish."

"You have to start somewhere."

Seth laughed. "I'll take the walk."

Tobias Beiler couldn't believe his good fortune. The Zook farm lay close to the Wyse property, so he could keep a close eye on Grace's movements without being seen. But first he had to get hired.

Deacon Zook was a small, rotund man with a no-nonsense look in his eye.

"Don't mean to be unfair, friend, but you look a mite old to take on as a hired man."

A flash of anger flared up in Tobias, but he reined it in and nodded. "Been wandering for a while, taking work where I can. No family, no children. My wife died, see, and, well, I just couldn't stand to stay on with memories of her around every corner . . ."

Tobias waited. Amish hospitality stretched further than initial impressions, and the sad story he'd fabricated was bound to touch the other man's heart. The deacon finally nodded and extended his hand. Tobias shook it heartily.

"We'll give it a whirl. I got one of the sheds fixed up as a bunkhouse, so you can stay there, take meals with the family." He named a more than fair sum for the wage and Tobias nodded.

"What do we call you? I'll introduce you to my wife and family."

Tobias paused for only a moment. "Abraham. Abraham Yoder."

Deacon Zook nodded. "Well, welcome then, Abraham. Please come inside."

Tobias nodded deferentially and entered the expansive kitchen with a faint smile.

CHAPTER 17

Violet set her chin as she stared at her sister. "I'm not up to anything."

"So you want to take a quilt square over to the Kings' for what reason?" Grace asked.

"I'm sure they could use it somehow. I heard at the wedding that they own one of the largest quilting frames around, and I am—"

"Not interested in quilting," Grace finished dryly. "But go anyway."

Violet beamed. "Great . . . *Danki.*"

Grace arched an eyebrow. "And say hello to Luke King for me. He cut quite a fine figure at the wedding."

Grace balanced on her cast and washed up the morning dishes. Seth was courteous and took his dishes to the sink for her; Abel did the same. And Violet barely ate, so anxious she was to get to the Kings'. She said a brief prayer that her sister might find a love worth keeping and one that would give her both *kinner* and a home richly full.

There was little for her to do in the big house except maintain its cleaning. Mary Wyse came over from the *daudi haus* to visit and wish Grace well, but Grace still could feel no true connection with her kind mother-in-law. She wondered if she would ever be able to trust completely, to accept the bishop's charge, to keep the pledge she'd made at her wedding.

She hobbled into the living room where Seth had set up her quilt frame when he hauled it over from her small house. Maybe she'd start a new pattern, give herself something to do. She never began a quilt without prayer—prayer to keep her from the sin of vanity, prayer to give her stamina to finish when her neck and arms begged for release, prayer for the one who would use the quilt.

But first, she needed inspiration.

She made her way out to the kitchen garden where zucchini and yellow squash rambled across the path. Rich red tomatoes, ripe for picking, drooped along the wire fence. Runner beans sprouted up higher than her head, and deep purple eggplants shone in the morning sun.

On the far edge of the garden, she rubbed a hand over the roughness of an oak tree's bark and thought about a quilt with dark browns in it; a quilt of strength, perhaps one for a man.

She bent to bury her nose in a pink hydrangea and saw the quilt softened by touches of mauve. She would start to piece it out tonight—the colors of the garden, the woods, the flowers.

Then she heard a strange zinging sound, and something heavy fell behind her on the garden path. She turned in time to see a large beehive, its angry occupants buzzing about in an awful horde.

And then she felt the first sting.

CHAPTER 18

Seth heard the shrieks as he crossed from the barn to the house. He followed the sound until he saw Grace among the flowers down by the gardens, her crutches flung aside, her arms flailing about her head. Then he realized what was happening and began to run.

He yanked his suspenders down and slid off his shirt as he moved through the garden. He reached her and flung the shirt over her head, lifting her off the ground as he ran the short distance to the house. Angry buzzing echoed in the quiet of the kitchen, and he swatted down the remaining bees that escaped from his shirt as he pulled it off Grace's head. He listened carefully, brushing down her clothes, until the silence was broken only by her choked sobs.

"The cast," she choked out. "I—I couldn't run."

He pulled three or four stingers out of the back of her neck, then dragged her closer to the light of a window. A particularly nasty sting was too deep for his fingers, and he automatically put his mouth over the area and began to suck to remove the stinger. He felt her grow still as he caught the stinger on his tongue, and then he realized what he was doing.

She half turned, staring up at him with wide lavender eyes, and he froze. He pulled the stinger from his mouth and rubbed at a stray curl of black hair that brushed her cheek.

"Grace? I'm sorry—some of the stingers are deep. It's best to get them out so the poison doesn't spread."

"I know."

He pulled her close and she gave in for a moment, infinitesimally relaxing against him. His heart hit his rib cage so hard that he couldn't breathe, and he eased his lips down toward her ear, murmuring in soothing tones.

Then he saw another red swelling beneath the edge of her *kapp* and reached for the stinger.

Suddenly she turned wild beneath his hands, twisting and turning away from him and catching at the sides of her prayer *kapp*.

"Grace, don't be stubborn. You've a stinger under your *kapp*."

"Seth, stop!"

"Grace, let me help you." He pulled once and the *kapp* fell into his hands. He caught his breath at what he saw. In that instant he realized that in the days since they'd been married, he'd never seen her without her *kapp*.

"I told you." She pushed past him and hurried as fast as she could out of the kitchen. He listened to the clatter of her footsteps up the stairs. He stared down at the prayer *kapp* in his fingers, then slowly sank to his knees on the floor.

"*Ach, Gott,*" he breathed.

Her hair—the lustrous black that peeped from the front of her prayer covering and matched the raven's wing of her brows—was shorn close to her head. Amish women normally grew their hair to heavy falls, a reminder that the Bible called a woman's hair her crowning glory. But Grace's hair had been mutilated and was now growing in tiny ringlets, like a boy's. He couldn't fathom why she would cut it—

And then it hit him with brutal force. Maybe she hadn't cut it at all.

Maybe Silas Beiler had.

Hobbling up the stairs on the stub of her cast, Grace staggered blindly into the first room she came to. The cool interior and the mixed smells of paint and linseed oil filled her senses like a balm of something distant and foreign. She needed treatment for the stings, but something about this room tantalized her with a sense of intimacy, an almost sacred pull.

She let her fingers trail over a still-damp palette of colors and moved to lift the edge of cloth covering a canvas.

CHAPTER 19

Luke King threw another fork of the pungent fresh hay into the stacked feeder. He relished the feel of his muscles at work, the scent of horse and hay and manure. He loved growing things, taking care of the land, tending the stock.

Farming let a man know where he stood.

The squeak of the barn door behind him caused him to jump. He thought he was alone.

Instead, here was that girl. The odd one from the wedding, who hid in the bushes. He dropped the pitchfork and squinted at her.

"What do you want?" he asked, the words coming out rougher than he meant.

"You," she said.

He blinked, then swiped his dirty hands on his loose white shirt. "Are you addled from the heat?"

She burst into merry laughter. "*Nee.* I mean what I say. I'm nineteen and looking for a man to love. From what I've gathered about you, I think you might fit the bill of sale."

He stared at her. Every other *Amisch* girl who'd gotten within ten yards of him had been demure, pleasant, and as distant as the *munn*. She took a step closer and he stepped back. She laughed again.

"Skittish, are you? Well, no matter. It's actually rather endearing."

"Look, Miss . . ."

"Violet," she prompted.

"Violet. Whatever. I am sweaty and dirty and look like a healthy farmer should. If I fit any bill of sale, it would be for a hired man." He lifted the pitchfork and held it in front of him. "If you'll excuse me, Miss—er, Violet, I've got work that needs doing."

She watched him with a calm, impassive gaze for a moment, then she nodded. "My intentions are clear, Luke King. I suggest you prepare for the onslaught." And then she spun on her heel and vanished into the slant of sunlight coming through the barn door.

Seth didn't move when he heard the kitchen door creak. He knew Jacob's footsteps. He stayed on his knees, feeling as if he'd run two miles and back. He shook his head.

"What's wrong?" Jacob said. "Where's Grace?"

Jacob put a hand on Seth's bare shoulder. Seth tried to hang on to the warmth of his brother's touch, but he felt lost, bereft for Grace's sake. And, he admitted to himself, for his own sake as well.

"Jacob, I think she's broken. Like a broken doll. I told you there were problems, but I didn't know how far—" He drew a sobbing breath, clutching the *kapp*, and looked up at his brother.

Jacob dropped to the floor in front of him. "*Was en de welt* is going on?"

"Her hair. I think he cut her hair."

"Who?"

"Silas Beiler. It was all hacked off, just starting to grow back, like—" He felt himself shiver despite the warmth of the summer day.

"Put your shirt on and get up. Where is she?"

"Upstairs."

Jacob got to his feet and handed Seth the white shirt. He slipped it over his head, then took Jacob's outstretched hand and pulled himself up.

"Go talk to her," Jacob said.

"She won't."

"If there's one thing I know about you, Seth Wyse, it's that you know how to get a woman talking. Now, go on."

"I've got to mix some baking soda paste first." He started to rummage around in the cupboards.

"What for?"

"Bee stings."

"Of course. Why didn't I guess?" Jacob shook his head and started for the door. "I'll go see to the horses."

Grace stared at the painting, mesmerized. It was a mountaintop scene that looked out onto a river valley. At the top of the mountain, facing away, stood a petite Amish woman and a small black-haired boy. The strength of the woman in the painting seemed to rival the mountains themselves.

Grace drew in a deep breath. It was, without a doubt, a portrayal of Abel and herself.

"It's not how I'd like to paint you."

Grace spun around to face her husband. His suspenders hung about his waist and his shirt was loose. He held a bowl of something white against his lean hip.

"You're not to paint me at all. It's a graven image. You know that."

Seth smiled at her. "Guilty as charged."

"But why would you risk it? You know that young man from Elk Valley was shunned recently for doing drawings."

"I've got some baking soda for the stings."

"Are you listening?" she cried. "Do you even care?"

"*Jah* and *jah*. But right now I'm concerned with those stings. So will you let me treat them?"

He set the bowl on top of the dresser and caught her hands in his own. She felt the warmth of his long fingers and did not resist as he eased her hands down. Then he was touching her hair, gently strumming through the strands, massaging her scalp here and there. He bent his broad back to kiss the short pieces, running his mouth close to her ear and then away, as if he was trying to heal her. She trembled at his gentleness, completely unused to such attention.

"Did he do this to you, Grace?"

She nodded, feeling a blush of shame heat her cheeks.

"Why?" The word was a hoarse whisper.

"He said my hair—my hair was a vanity. He cut it every year." She reached for the bowl. "Please—the stings. I'll tend to them myself."

He let her go abruptly and moved to the front of the painting. She watched him run his fingers over the damp palette, touching the colors, almost as if she had disappeared. She clutched the bowl and was edging past him when he looked at her.

He slid two fingers into his pocket and pulled out the squashed *kapp*. "Don't forget this."

"*Danki*," she whispered.

She glanced down at the *kapp*, now smudged by the paint from his fingertips. It seemed fitting, as if he were making a statement—branding her as his own, somehow.

A tightness clutched at her chest. Her breath came in short gasps. Without looking at him, she jerked the *kapp* onto her head and hurried out of the room.

Never again would she allow herself to be captured by a man.

Any man.

CHAPTER 20

Seth fooled with the painting for about half an hour, feeling his heart rate slowly settle as he tinkered. He had been turned upside down inside by Grace's nearness, by the silken feel of her hair. He wiped his hands on a rag and decided it was time to head back to work. Jacob had to be wondering where he was.

When he went downstairs, he saw Grace through the back kitchen window, splotches of white on her neck and cheek, a proper *kapp* back in place as she hung up sheets on the line. He decided he didn't want to press her right now with his presence and headed out the front door instead, only to encounter Abel sitting in the dust at the front of the steps.

He stooped down next to the boy and watched the intensity with which the child drew something on the ground with a stick. Seth cocked his head, sensing it was better to observe than interrupt. He studied the picture on the ground. It was a basic tree with a heavy branch extending from its side. There was a large protrusion hanging from the branch. In the next drawing, a stick figure waved its arms wildly around its head while stick flowers bent at its feet. Seth saw a drop of moisture hit the ground and realized that Abel was crying.

"Hey," he said softly, touching the child's shoulder. "What is it?"

Abel shook his head, the tears coming faster now. Seth sensed he was gathering energy to bolt and spoke quickly.

"Abel, remember when you came to me and Jacob about the bad man? We helped you, right?"

Abel nodded after a long moment.

"Then let me help you now. You can tell me anything." *But then again, maybe he couldn't. Maybe the drawing is the telling.*

Seth studied the outlines more closely, and the figure waving its arms suddenly clicked in his brain. Grace in the garden with the bees. Had the boy seen his mother get hurt?

"Abel, your *mamm* is *gut*. She's hanging out clothes right now. She got a few stings, but she's all right. Did you see her?"

"I did it!" the child burst out, flinging the stick across the ground and scrambling to his feet. He was off like a shot, and Seth dashed after him. He'd played this game before and was not about to let the boy get out of sight.

Abel rounded the house and Seth followed. They passed Grace, who looked up in alarm. She started to move toward them, but Seth waved her off. "Hiya! Having some quality bonding time, that's all!"

The kid was fast, but Seth's long legs covered the ground easily—until they entered the cornfield.

The stalks were high, and Abel left little imprint of his passage. Seth sighed in frustration, then hollered for the boy. There were rattlesnakes in the field as well as the normal corn and black snakes.

"Abel! Come on, please!" He stood on tiptoe and caught the slightest waver in the silken tops about ten feet ahead and to his left. He plunged into the corn and saw the flash of a small black pant leg. He pressed on and finally caught the child, who squawked and kicked furiously.

"Don't run and I'll let you down."

Abel stilled, and Seth lowered him to the ground between the cornstalks.

"All right. Now, what do you mean, *you did it*?"

Abel shifted restlessly and caught hold of a cornstalk. "I had my slingshot and I was by the garden and I saw this big thing hanging down from the tree. I shot at it and it fell down by Mama. But I didn't see her until too late. It was my fault."

The child began to sob. Seth dropped to his knees in front of him, catching him close. He felt the tension in the small body and then the release as he let his weight rest briefly against Seth.

"It was an accident, Abel."

"I'm scared."

"Don't be. Nothing bad is going to happen to you. You're very brave to tell me the truth." Seth thought for a moment, then caught the boy's small hand. "Listen, Abel, come with me. I want to tell you a story."

Grace had to resist the urge to follow her husband when he passed by with Abel, giving her only a brief wave. She was pleased to see Abel's hand in Seth's.

As she went back to pinning clothes to the clothes-line, a fly buzzed past. She jumped and swatted, then laughed at herself when she saw it wasn't a bee. She stretched one of Seth's broad white shirts on the line and smoothed it with her hands.

There was a time when marriage to a man like Seth would have been the culmination of all her dreams. He was perfect—well, nearly so, if you didn't count the painting. Why did she have to second-guess herself all the time? Why couldn't she just be thankful to *der Herr* for what He had given her?

She set another clothespin and took in a sharp breath. Deep inside, she had to admit that she'd struggled on a soul level with God since her marriage to Silas. She couldn't help feeling as if God had set a trap for her, that the whole thing was either a cruel joke or, at best, a faulty plan. Still, she knew that der Herr had plans *not to harm her but to give her hope and a future.*

Was Seth Wyse part of that plan? She couldn't tell. God's voice seemed faint and far away.

"Where is Seth?"

Jacob's voice made her jump, and she swatted through the damp clothes to see her brother-in-law.

"*Ach*, he took Abel inside a bit ago. I don't know why. I can go and see."

"*Nee*, never mind. You're bee-stung. Are you all right?"

"I'm fine, *danki*."

"I was thinking maybe you and Abel and Seth could come over for dinner one night?"

"Uh, *jah*. We will."

"When?"

Grace hid a smile. Jacob was so blunt, while Seth tended to be cryptic in what he said.

"Whenever you like."

"Tomorrow night, then. Thursday. Bring Violet too, if she wants to come. I'll tell Lilly."

Grace had to laugh. "Don't you think you should ask Lilly first?"

Jacob smiled, and for once she could see the similarity between the two brothers. "Lilly's fine with it. She's been waiting to ask but wanted to give you time alone too."

"Well, then we'll be glad to come."

"*Gut*. Tell Seth I'm meeting a buyer out at the corral. A woman."

"All right," Grace said. She wondered why Jacob had emphasized that the horse buyer was a woman. Then with a shrug she dropped a last clothespin into the bag and headed off to see what Seth and Abel were doing.

CHAPTER 21

Seth opened the door to his old bedroom and art studio. He lifted the painting down and set it on the floor against the wall. Then he put a fresh canvas onto the easel. He turned to Abel.

"Did you know I like to read, Abel?"

The boy shrugged, his eyes drifting about the room.

"I've read a lot of stories about very brave men going into battle."

"We're not supposed to fight."

"You're absolutely right. We're not. But we can learn something from these men. They often prayed to be brave, and then they would paint their faces."

Seth knew he had the child's full attention and curiosity by the way his eyes grew wide.

"Why paint on their faces?"

"Some people called it 'war paint.'" Seth took his palette and mixed a little blue tempera powder with a few drops of the clean water he kept in a jug on the shelf.

"But war is bad . . ."

"Suppose we called it something else—not war paint, but bravery paint? A way of showing on the outside the courage you can feel inside. I know you remember bad things from your *fater*, Abel, but that's over. You got through it—you're brave and strong."

He dipped a finger in the paint and reached his hand to Abel's cheek. The boy didn't flinch when Seth drew a line of blue across his skin.

"You really think I'm brave?"

Seth clenched his jaw at the quiver in the child's voice and marked his other cheek. "*Jah*, Abel. And you can be brave and tell me anything you want, anything you remember, anytime."

"I remember a lot."

Seth nodded and laid the palette aside.

"*Nee!*" Abel cried suddenly. "You do it too, Seth. You're brave too."

"All right." Seth stared into the mirror of the child's eyes and drew the blue lines across his own face.

"We're the same now," Abel said. He ran his fingers back and forth across a fan brush.

"*Jah*, the same, *sohn*." He said the last word without thinking and felt his eyes well up with tears. But Abel didn't seem to notice. Seth swallowed hard.

"Can I paint?" Abel asked.

"*Jah*, of course you can."

"No! He cannot!"

The words exploded from the depths of Grace's being. She had been standing outside the doorway, listening, feeling her heart throb at Seth's tenderness. Painting, however, was not something she could allow.

But she was also amazed that she had dared to

contradict her husband. She knew it was not good for a child to see parents at odds—it was one reason she had been compliant with whatever Silas wished. But there were other reasons too.

Was it possible that she could argue with Seth and not get hurt?

Seth bowed his head slightly toward her with a frown, but his words were calm and sure. "Abel, go outside and work at weeding the kitchen garden. Pretty can watch you. And wear your paint proudly. There's no one to see anyway, so don't worry about looking funny."

"Are you keeping yours on, Seth?"

"For a little while. Now, obey your *mamm*. There will be other times to paint."

Abel went to his mother. "I'm brave, *Mamm*. See my face?"

She touched his dark hair gently. "Very brave, my love." Abel nodded, and his footsteps echoed on the treads as he went downstairs.

Grace clutched her hands together, waiting to see what her husband would say to her.

"In case you're wondering, it's only tempera paint. It won't hurt him, and it washes off." He picked up a rag and wiped the blue paint off his fingers. "How long were you there?"

"Long enough to hear what you said to him. I thank you."

"There's no need to be so stiff and formal, Grace. I understand that you don't want him to paint, but with a kid like Abel—well, painting might give him an outlet for his thoughts and feelings. I caught him drawing in the dirt outside."

"That's different," she said.

He smiled grimly and walked to her. "Is it really? It's art. Primitive, perhaps, but still art."

"I don't understand you—what you want. Why you're willing to risk offending the community by—"

He ran his finger across his face and reached out in a flash to swipe her cheek blue.

"What . . . what are you doing?"

"Brave, Grace Wyse. You're very brave, and I admire you."

She floundered for a moment and he wet her other cheek, then stepped so close that his legs brushed her skirts. She resisted the urge to step back.

"That's right, my brave wife," he whispered. "No backing away."

"I don't want Abel to paint."

"I know." He bent close enough to whisper the words in her ear, and for just an instant touched his cheek to her own. She couldn't breathe for a moment. She understood what he was trying to say—that they were together, their bravery, their strength as one.

But the intensity of the moment overwhelmed her, and she fled from him to their bedroom. She looked at herself hesitantly in the small bureau mirror and then felt the smeared blue paint on her cheek with wonder.

Silas had always been careful not to mar her face in any way; he worried what others would think, she supposed. But never had he touched her with anything approaching tenderness. Never had she known such intimacy as she had with Seth.

She dipped a cotton cloth into the washbasin on the dresser and was just about to wipe away the color when something stopped her. Instead she sank onto the bed and began to pray.

Ach, dear Gott, *help me to find some thread of myself to offer to this new husband—this one who would be a* fater *in truth to Abel. Help me to forget the past, to trust. Bless Seth and help me, help me to indeed be brave and to bring honor to this marriage and family.*

Then she straightened her spine and wiped off the paint with clean strokes. But she could still feel its mark and the warmth of Seth's cheek, blending them into a togetherness that was rich with promise.

CHAPTER 22

"Come here a minute, will you, Seth?" Jacob asked formally. "Miss Mason—if you'll give us a second?" Jacob had hold of Seth's arm and was steering him toward the barn and away from the corral.

"What?" Seth asked.

"You've got blue paint on your cheeks."

"*Ach*, I thought I got it all off." Seth swiped an arm across his face.

"I don't want to know why you're painting your face, but this buyer is going to think you're a weird Amish man doing some weird Amish thing."

"I'll go wash my face. Just keep her busy."

"Yeah, right."

Seth laughed. His brother hated this aspect of the horse-selling business—the women. Sure, there were male customers too, but there were also a lot of curious women. In this case, Jennifer Mason was blond, interested, and a rich daddy's daughter.

"Listen," Jacob said. "Behave yourself around this one, all right? You don't want Grace to see anything."

"What is there to see exactly, Jacob?"

His brother sighed. "Seth, you're a born flirt, and you know it."

Seth chuckled. Women were too much for Jacob, who had been hounded by females for years before marrying Lilly. "Maybe you should do the flirting, then."

Jacob gave a snort. "Nobody's flirting. We're both married men, in case you need reminding. Now, mind what I say."

Seth watched him stalk off, then ducked into the barn to scrub hastily at his face again with lye soap and a bucket of water.

Grace left the porch with a new determination in her heart, a commitment to try harder with Seth. Her steps slowed when she saw the young woman talking with Jacob in the near corral. She had long, loose blond hair and wore a tight pink T-shirt, curvy blue jeans, and boots.

Grace felt sure that Lilly would have a fit if she saw how the woman casually reached out and touched Jacob's arm. Not that Jacob looked too happy about it. Then she saw her husband walk over to them, and Seth was smiling and shaking the girl's hand.

Grace approached the corral in time to see the other woman link her arm through Seth's. She felt a peculiar catch in her chest. She went to the fence railing and tried to act casual.

"Hi, Seth, Jacob. I thought your guest might like a glass of tea."

Three pairs of eyes swung in her direction, and the woman, barely more than a teenager, flashed her a perfect smile. "Oh, how neat. A real Amish lady. I think your dress is so cool! But don't you get hot?"

Grace tried to follow the jabbering train of words and murmured softly as Seth sought to disentangle himself from the girl's arm.

"Uh, this is—my wife, Grace. Grace, this is Jennifer Mason. She's looking to buy a little mare to ride."

"Yeah," the girl gushed. "My daddy's nineteenth birthday present, you know? I wanted a car, but I like to ride. I can't believe you two are together. I mean, your skin is beautiful, Grace, but you look older than Seth. Are there Amish women who like younger men? There's a lot of women like that around where I live and—"

"How about that tea, Grace?" Seth interrupted.

Grace clenched the fence rail with white-tipped fingers and blinked in the bold sunlight. "Of course. I suppose I'm still spry enough to get it." The *Englisch* girl's words roiled in her head. No doubt she was used to saying what she thought—she was young and beautiful and naïve and probably meant no harm in her casual talk. But to be noticed as being older—what must other *Amisch* think?

"Please, come inside when you've finished. I'll have the tea ready."

Violet heard Grace come in, slamming the screen door behind her. She went and peered through the screen. "Who's that wild-looking girl out there?"

"A *customer*."

Violet didn't miss the irony in her sister's tone. "You mean a *young* customer, right? Young, rich, and beautiful. I'd be jealous."

Grace frowned at her. "Why would you be jealous? You're stunning and she's a—well . . ."

Violet laughed and came to link an arm around her sister's slim waist. "If I'm stunning, then I wonder what to call you, since I'm only a shadow of your beauty."

"*Ach*, Violet, go on with you. I've got to fetch that— girl—some tea."

Violet gave her an impish look. "I could serve it for you, but I bet tea stains bleach-blond hair."

Grace laughed and Violet darted happily away, glad she'd been able to cheer her sister somewhat.

"I warned you," Jacob said as he spread wax on a saddle.

It was almost lunchtime. The sale had gone well, with Jennifer Mason paying top dollar for a spirited mare. But tea with Grace had not been the brightest spot in the day.

"I didn't do anything," Seth protested, filling feeders with grain. But he knew what was coming because he'd felt it in his heart.

"That girl was all over you, and you let her hurt Grace."

"Well, what exactly was I supposed to say, Jacob? The girl talked a mile a minute and Grace would have been embarrassed if I'd protested. By the way, do you think there is that much difference in our appearances?"

Jacob rolled his eyes. "What is wrong with you?"

"I'm serious."

"That's what worries me. Why don't you focus on

going in and making your wife feel like age doesn't matter?"

"*Ach*, all right," he said.

"Hey, you three are coming for dinner tomorrow night. Bring Violet too, if she wants."

"Really? You got Grace to accept? How'd you do that?" Seth asked.

Jacob gave him a smug smile. "I used my charm."

CHAPTER 23

Grace looked down to find that the carrot she had been scraping for the fresh vegetable plate was whittled down to nearly nothing. With a sigh of disgust, she dropped it into the compost bin and picked up another.

If only she could forget the morning. When she gazed out the kitchen window, all she saw was Abel playing happily with Pretty, but she couldn't rid herself of the image of Jennifer Mason—the blond hair, tight jeans, and flirty manner. Coy, confident, and calculatingly candid.

She kept telling herself that a few years' difference really did not matter, but she was resolved to find out Seth's exact age once and for all.

She looked up in surprise as he came through the back door. He paused to stare at her, then moved past her to wash his hands at the sink. She went to the screen door to call Abel.

"Come on in, *sohn*. Lunchtime," she said. "I made apple strudel."

"Oh boy, my favorite!" Abel cried.

"Mine too," Seth said.

Grace got a sudden impulse and smiled. "All right then, let's have apple strudel first, before soup and vegetables."

"What?" Seth and Abel asked in unison.

"You heard me."

Man and boy raced to the table. Grace brought over three plates and then the pan of crusty apple goodness. Just as she finished serving everyone, there was a knock at the door. Grace rose to answer it, hoping that another female horse buyer wasn't at the door. But it was her mother- and father-in-law.

"You never have to knock. You are always welcome here." She held the door wide. "Please come in. We're having dessert—before lunch."

Seth got up to hug his parents while Abel continued to eat the apple strudel. Mary and Samuel joined them at the table, and Grace brought extra plates. As she watched the older couple, she wondered what it would be like to be visiting in a home where you had raised your children and lived for so long.

Still, she was grateful for the space and the privacy—both for herself and for Abel. The truth was that the boy could be odd, and even as loving as her new in-laws were, she was concerned about revealing the true nature of her son to people. Grace was never ashamed of him, but she did sometimes feel embarrassed.

She looked down the table at him now. He still had blue paint streaks on his cheeks and was happily stuffing himself with strudel.

"This is delicious," Mary said.

"*Danki.*"

Samuel cleared his throat, breaking into her thoughts.

"There's a new mare I'd like you to look at with me in town, Seth."

"Sure thing." He turned toward Grace. "Can the soup wait for supper?"

She nodded. "It just gets better with simmering."

"Great. We'll bring Abel along too."

Abel looked up from his plate and grinned at the prospect. Grace tried to push down the alarm that rose up inside her. She had never let Abel go very far from her, but Seth was her husband and Abel's new father.

"Please be careful," she said to Seth.

"Of course." He bent to kiss her forehead and used the distraction to swipe the last bite of strudel from her plate. She hugged her son briefly, then watched him slip his hand into Seth's and head out the door.

Grace turned to Mary in the sudden hollowness of the kitchen. "I don't feel right here sometimes," she said. "This is your place, your home. You should be here."

"No," Mary said. "I was glad to move to the *daudi haus*, and I am looking forward to the time when we will have other grand-children—in addition to Abel. We love him like our own, you know."

"I know. Thank you."

As they talked, Grace felt her spirit relax within her. The closest she'd ever come to an adult mother-daughter relationship was with Alice Miller. She had been barely out of childhood when she had married Silas, and he had kept her isolated from seeing her family. She had missed all the joy of becoming friends with her mother. And now *Mamm* was gone, and that void could never be filled.

"I wonder about other children too," she confessed.

Mary smiled. "What do you imagine a child of yours and Seth's would be like?"

Grace swallowed. "*Ach*, blue eyes and that laughing smile, tiny white teeth and golden hair."

"Not black hair and those unusual eyes of yours?" Mary said.

In truth, it never occurred to Grace to think of her own violet eyes or dark hair. She rarely thought of herself at all. And she certainly never shared such personal feelings with anyone else.

Perhaps life was changing for her, after all.

Seth let his *daed* drive as they made their way into town. It was only three miles to Lockport, and Seth enjoyed spending time with his father.

"Well, *sohn*, how is married life?"

Seth glanced behind him in the buggy. Abel had fallen asleep against Pretty. The rhythm of the drive always soothed the child somehow.

Seth sighed. "Hard," he admitted quietly. "Grace is such a complex person—there are so many layers to her that I can't seem to fathom. It's like throwing a rock into a deep pond and knowing you're never really going to see it touch bottom. I don't know what to do with her sometimes."

His father laughed. "Welcome to the world of women. Even with your *mamm*, it took me two years of marriage to figure out some things—that she didn't like turnips or the way I hung shirts on the line upside down."

"You hung shirts?" Seth tried to remember if he'd ever seen his father doing laundry. He was used to *Daed* dealing with the horses. It was hard to imagine him doing domestic chores.

"Sure," his dad went on. "You've got to help. The family is the center—remember that."

"I know," Seth said. "But she doesn't let me near her."

His father was quiet for a moment, then spoke thoughtfully. "Grace is a woman with a past. I can feel it in my bones. She has lived a hard life and yet has a beautiful spirit."

"*Danki, Daed*," Seth said.

They soon made the turn into Lockport and drove to a corral just outside of town. There an *Englischer* had a spirited palomino mare. In an obviously misguided attempt to calm her down, he struck the mare forcefully with his quirt. She reared against the lead, thrashing to get away from the whip.

Before Seth could stop him, Abel jumped off the back of the wagon, slipped under the fence, and ran toward the horse and the man. All Seth could see was slashing hooves and the lashing whip, and sheer terror gripped his heart as he dashed after the boy.

Then everything stopped. Abel's hand was on the mare, and she was standing quietly under his touch. In one simple second, everything was calm and right.

Seth felt his heart pounding in his ears as he stared at Abel. The dumbstruck *Englischer* dropped the whip. Seth felt his father's steadying touch on his shoulder.

"I've never seen anything like that," the *Englisch* man said. He stared at the boy and the horse. "That kid ought to go on one of them animal whisperer TV shows they got."

Seth looked at Abel, and the boy smiled as he ran his hands along the horse's flanks. "You don't hit," Abel said.

"*Nee*, that's right, *sohn*," Seth said.

The *Englisch* man came over with an extended hand. "Maybe the kid's got something. I sure didn't know how to calm her down."

Seth and his father shook hands with the man quietly. They made a deal for the mare, not giving in to the man's exorbitant fee, but bargaining until a fair price was reached.

Samuel glanced at the sky as they finished. "What do you boys say to some lunch? That apple strudel was good, but I'm still hungry."

The *Englisch* man declined but agreed to keep the mare in the corral until they were done in town. Seth got in the buggy and stared straight ahead. "You ever see anything like that before, *Daed*?" he whispered.

His father lifted the reins. "Nope. Not ever. That boy's something special."

CHAPTER 24

I've decided I'm going to do a honeybee quilt," Grace told Mary Wyse. "Browns and yellows and rich and warm colors, as if for a man."

"Perhaps a certain man?"

"Well, maybe. Seth likes art and creative things, but I guess you know that."

Mary nodded fondly. "*Jah*, it's been our family's secret. Perhaps we should have told the bishop, but something in me would not break Seth's spirit when he found such joy in the painting. As a child he spent money that he had worked for on art supplies—walked all the way into Lockport to buy a watercolor set and some paper. He kept the drawings under his bed, but finally I found them one day. When I confronted him, he started to cry. I knew I could not take it away from him. Jacob, too, has been fierce in protecting him with his art."

Grace hesitated. Mary's words shamed her. She had not exactly been protective of her husband's art.

"So, shall we start this quilt?" Mary asked.

"Well," Grace said, "I always pray before I begin any quilt. Would you pray with me?"

"Of course." Mary stretched her hand across the fabric pieces.

Grace loved the feel of Mary's skin—weathered from work, but strong and warm. Grace began to pray out loud quietly.

"Dear *Gott*, thank You for this talent, this chance to serve You in making a quilt. I pray for the design, that it would be of Your making and not of my own mind. I pray for time to finish. I pray for those it covers, that You would gently lead them closer to You, and that You would grant them grace through the threads of the quilt itself."

"I didn't understand before how you came up with such beautiful designs," Mary said. "But now I know that *der Herr* has a hand in it."

Grace ducked her head.

Mary laughed. "I know we're taught that praise is vanity, but as a mother I cannot help myself."

As a mother. Grace cherished those words. Her own mother had been dead for almost six months now, and Grace hadn't even known it until Violet brought her the news. How strange, to think of someone you love as alive, only to find out they had passed on. Raw grief welled up in her, and regret.

After Silas's death she could have gone back. But she had been in such a hurry to flee the property, to get away to a place where Tobias couldn't find her. And perhaps, just a little, she resented her parents' decision in sending her to Silas in the first place.

Whatever the cause, she had left Middle Hollow without contacting her family. Now it seemed like a foolish choice. But it was too late.

The drift of her thoughts disturbed her, and she chose instead to concentrate on putting the brown and yellow percale pieces together. She had in mind the pattern of a honeybee hive and the motion of flight, and she let the natural rhythm of stitching take over.

"So how is marriage?" Mary asked. "I don't mean to be nosy. I just thought you might like to talk."

Grace felt her mother-in-law's kind eyes upon her across the expanse of the fabric. She carefully pulled a thread through before answering.

"It's good," she said.

"I hope that I have raised my *sohns* to cherish their wives."

"Oh, I am cherished," Grace said.

She longed to talk to this woman who was her mother-in-law. But how could she explain that she didn't even feel married to Seth? It certainly wasn't something a mother would want to hear.

Samuel Wyse drove the buggy through Lockport, and Seth's eyes strayed to the passing storefronts. Emily's Mystery—Seth knew from his brother's experience that it was a place with pretty underthings for a wife, the kind that would please a man. Seth dragged his eyes away from the store. He hadn't done more than kiss his wife on the forehead, and thinking about kissing was not something he wanted to do while he was with his father.

They drove up to Pinky's Restaurant and tied up at the hitching post. Pinky's was a hole-in-the-wall place that served both *Amisch* and *Englisch*. It was filled with neon lights and an old jukebox that was playing "The Candy Man." They found a booth, and Seth watched Abel as the boy stared at the lights, utterly fascinated.

Pinky greeted them himself, a tall *Englisch* man with a pencil-thin moustache. His place sold the best burgers and fries around, and he knew it. He greeted Samuel and Seth with a smile.

"Heard you got married," Pinky said.

"Yep," Seth agreed. "This is my boy, Abel."

Abel barely nodded in greeting as he stared at the flashing Christmas lights draped along the wall. They soon dug into the fries and the juicy burgers; it was not usual Amish fare but was delicious nonetheless.

"Seth, can I go look around at the lights?" Abel asked when he had finished most of his burger.

"*Jah*, go ahead," Seth said. He was glad to get a little uninterrupted time with his dad. When Abel had wandered off, Seth drained the last of his milk shake and turned to his father. "So, tell me more about women."

Samuel smiled. "Seth, I'd say to be respectful of the promise you made at your wedding and you'll be fine."

But Seth couldn't remember the promise, no matter how hard he wracked his brain and tried to relive the wedding ceremony. At last Pinky put him out of his misery with another round of milk shakes and some more local gossip.

Abel returned to the table. He studied the last French fry on Seth's thick plate.

"You want the last bite?" Seth asked, tilting his plate. He was surprised when Abel looked at him with shock.

"No, it's a baby French fry. Please can you wrap it up and I take it home to Mama?"

Seth saw that the boy was completely serious.

"All riiiight." Seth started to fold the fry in a napkin and Abel shook his head.

"*Nee*, wrap it like a baby, Seth, please."

Seth cast one eye at his impassive father and proceeded to swaddle the fry, leaving only the tip sticking out. "Like that?"

"Yep." Abel took the fry as gently as he would have a baby, cradling it in his hand. "*Danki*."

Soon they were riding back home, with the new mare walking calmly behind on a lead.

"You gonna tell Grace about the little horse incident?" Samuel asked.

"Should I?"

Samuel laughed. "Not if you want to take that boy into town again."

"You're right, *Daed*," Seth said. "Some things are better left a mystery."

He glanced back at Abel cradling the French fry and suspected his words were truer than he could possibly imagine.

CHAPTER 25

Alice breathed a sigh of relief as the blue van finally roared to a blaring stop in front of the big white farmhouse. She tried to express her thanks to Tommy but couldn't manage to shout loud enough over his music. He was ready to pull away, so she clambered down, carrying the simple brown suitcase and her Pink Lady cosmetics bag.

Grace came off the porch with slow steps. And then the two women were embracing and laughing. Alice thrilled to the generous touch. Despite her friends' best intentions, she hadn't been truly hugged since Bud had gone.

"What happened to you?" Alice said, pointing to Grace's cast.

Grace shrugged. "Broken ankle. I was working in the garden and the wall came down on me. I'll be out of it in another week."

"Honey, I'm so sorry."

"It's all right. I'm used to the cast. I get around just fine, don't even need the crutches." She waved her friend's concern away. "Alice, I'm so sorry about Bud."

"Oh, thank you, Grace. I've been so lonely, and

I thought some time with you might restore me a bit. Bud's in heaven, and I'll be free to join him soon enough with this tired old body." Alice let her gaze wander to the third-story windows. "Now, I thought you were living in some small cabin or another. This is a fine house."

"I got married," Grace said.

Alice raised a finely made-up brow. "Married? I would have thought you'd never entertain such an idea again after . . ."

Grace nodded. "I know—it's strange how God worked it out. But please come in. I'll explain."

"Wait." Alice put a hand on her arm. "Will your new husband mind me being here?"

"Not a bit. My sister, Violet, is here too," Grace said.

"Now, this is bright and cheery," Alice said when Grace ushered her inside. "Not like that prison you lived in before. I remember Silas's window blinds—the darkness of that place. Windows closed, blinds closed, curtains closed."

"All the better to shroud his wife and son," Grace muttered.

"Now, now," Alice said. "I got you thinking of the past, Grace. Stop it. I want to see what this new man is like."

At that moment a tall, handsome man walked in the door.

Grace smiled at him. "Seth, this is Alice Miller, my friend."

"Hiya!" Seth took off his hat and made a little bow in Alice's direction.

"Hi yourself," Alice said. She arched an eyebrow in Grace's direction.

Seth picked up her bag. "Front bedroom?" he asked Grace. "By the way, town went great—Abel was a treat. He's outside playing."

Grace nodded. Once he was gone, Alice said, "He's hot, honey."

"I guess."

"You guess? I'd think you'd know, since you're married to the man."

Grace shrugged. "Abel has been sleeping with us since we got married."

Alice stared at her. "So you're telling me that you have been living in the house with that specimen of a man and you have been having Abel sleep between you?"

"And the dog," Grace added.

"Oh, honey, you have been needing me."

CHAPTER 26

Seth set the suitcase down in the front bedroom. Alice Miller looked like a comfortable kind of woman, and Violet was young and energetic and great with Abel. Maybe both women would help Grace come out of her shell a bit.

He headed toward the stairs, and as he passed his old bedroom, he noticed that the door was slightly ajar. He thought Abel was outside, but here he was, painting on a new canvas. He must have used the back stairs and come up to paint instead.

Abel had chosen bright primary colors: blue, red, orange, and yellow. The child had a masterful stroke of the brush; he was painting with feeling, his small jaw clenched with an emotion Seth suspected might be anger, or maybe fear.

Seth understood the sacredness of art and personal space. He started to back quietly out of the room. Then Abel turned to look at him.

"I'm sorry, Seth." The boy bit his lip and let the brush sag downward.

"For what?"

"Mama said no painting, but your room was open, and I saw the paints, and I just wanted to try."

Seth nodded. "I understand. Can you tell me what this painting is about?"

Abel shrugged. "I don't know. It's about me inside."

Seth wanted to push a little bit more but did not want to frighten the child. "Abel, can you tell me about the red in the painting? What does the red mean?"

"Red is mad," Abel said. "Mad, mad, mad."

Seth nodded. "*Jah*, sometimes we use red when we're upset or passionate."

"What's pash'nate?"

"It means we really care about something. What do you really care about, Abel?"

The boy's face scrunched as he thought, and for a minute Seth didn't think he was going to respond. "Mama," he said finally. "I want to keep Mama safe."

"She is safe," Seth said.

"Maybe. Maybe."

Seth stooped down next to the boy and whispered softly, "Abel, you can come here and paint anytime you want."

"Really?"

"Yep. I'll talk to your mother. Remember, anytime you want. Now, put that brush in the water if you've finished. You should always clean your brushes."

Seth had a million questions going around in his head that he wanted to ask about Silas Beiler, about what kind of a father he had been to the boy. But Abel couldn't describe the picture in more dynamic terms, and Seth wouldn't pressure the boy to say bad things about his father. He closed the door gently on the boy and headed back down the stairs.

He gave a passing grin to Alice, who eyed him like he was something to have on a plate. Seth was used to this kind of behavior from women, young and old, so he just laughed it off. Grace, however, looked uncomfortable, and he went to her side.

"How are you doing?" he asked.

"Fine. We're fine," Grace said.

Fine. Such an empty word.

Violet breezed through the kitchen, declined the strudel, introduced herself to Alice, and then flitted off again.

"That girl's up to something," Grace muttered to no one in particular.

"Well, okay then, I'll get back to work." Seth went out the kitchen door. He couldn't bring himself at the moment to tell Grace about Abel's painting, so he went down the field to bring up Grace's horse, Amy, who had thrown a shoe.

He fired up the smithy and put the new shoe into the coals, but he was thinking about Grace rather than paying attention. When he went to pick it up, he accidentally touched one side of the hot tongs. He plunged his hand into the cooling bucket, and when he pulled it out, the burn was already puckering.

He looked at the horse. "Well, Amy, you have your new shoe and I have a burn." He supposed that he should go back to the house, clean it, and wrap it. On the positive side, Grace might give him some tender sympathy— which would be more than worth a stinging burn.

Grace sat at the table with Alice, and they talked about baking and quilting. Alice was an excellent quilter, even for an *Englisch* woman. Grace explained her design about the honeybees—the hive pattern and the yellow and browns that would suit a male room. Alice was pleased.

"What a great idea! So you got stung by the bees?"

"Yes."

"And your husband got the stingers out?"

Grace felt her cheeks flood with color and she nodded.

Alice laughed. "Well then, maybe it was worth a few stings."

Abel came humming downstairs then. He had his hands behind his back.

"Abel, what are you up to?" Grace said. "I thought you were outside."

"Nothing." He went to the sink and started to wash his hands. Grace came over and saw the colors red and blue mix with the water from the washing basin.

"Abel? Were you painting? Were you in Seth's paint?"

The child looked up at her with some alarm. "*Jah*, but Seth said I could."

"Seth *said* you could?"

"I'm sorry, *Mamm*."

Grace sighed. "It's okay. Go outside and play with Pretty."

"So, if you don't mind me asking, what is wrong with painting?" Alice looked at her from the table. "I know that the Amish are concerned about graven images—no faces and no photographs and all of that— but surely painting a simple picture without any people is not a big deal, is it?"

Grace shook her head. "I don't know what the bishop would think."

"Well, isn't it more important what God thinks? If Abel likes art and can express himself through it—because Lord knows that the boy doesn't talk much—this might be just what he needs."

Grace bowed her head. "Maybe you're right, but I—" She broke off as Seth came in the door with his hand cradled in front of him.

"What happened?"

"Only a burn," he said cheerfully. "No big deal. I was being careless at the smithy and lost my train of thought."

Grace took him by the arm and led him to the basin of water, now clouded a vaguely purple color from the blue and red paint.

Seth cleared his throat. "I guess we need clean water."

"Yes," Grace said. "Abel just washed his hands."

"I'll go see if Abel remembers me and meet that pup of his." Alice jumped up and left the kitchen, banging the screen door behind her.

"I didn't encourage him to do it," Seth said. "The boy found it of his own accord, and I will not dissuade him. It might give him a chance to open up, Grace, to speak in a way that he can't speak. If you want to know what was in the painting, you should look at it. There was anger and passion and—"

"That's enough," Grace snapped.

There was a tense silence for a moment, then Grace went on in a shaky voice. "I asked one thing, that Abel not paint, and you promised. You broke that promise."

"I never promised," Seth said.

"You put your cheek to mine, you made a pact," Grace cried. Then she caught herself and said, "I'm sorry for speaking so abruptly. Please forgive me."

"There's nothing to forgive," Seth said. "Grace, you have to understand that you can talk back to me. You can say what you want. I will not hurt you. This is a different world."

"No," she said, leaning wearily against the sink. "It's really not."

She poured out the basin of cloudy water and filled it with fresh water from the pitcher, then drew his hand down into the cool bowl. "It's really not a different world if I don't have a say, if I don't have a place to feel and to think and to make decisions about my son. And he is my son."

Seth looked at her and she felt the intensity of his gaze. "I don't take that lightly, Grace. I love him." He stopped and then looked at her again, a gentle smile playing about his lips. "Grace, let me adopt Abel. Please. We can go into Lockport to the courthouse and do the adoption papers. I want him to be Abel Wyse. I want him to be my son in truth."

Grace swished her hands in the water and gazed down at their hands linked together in the basin. The issue of the painting wasn't over, she knew. But marriage required compromise, and she very much wanted Abel to have Seth's name.

"I'd like that," she said.

"Would Abel mind?"

"I don't know if he would understand."

"Then let's talk to him," Seth said. "And let's talk more about the painting later."

The screen door banged open. Alice came in, followed by Abel, who held out a fistful of fresh daisies to his mother. She took them gracefully.

"Abel and I have been talking," Alice said. "And Abel is going to come in my room tonight. I told him I get scared in this big old house, and he offered to sleep beside me—with Pretty, even."

"Oh no, I don't want him to disturb you—" Grace began.

But Seth cut her off. "I think it's a great idea."

CHAPTER 27

Nighttime came on faster than Grace would have liked. She delayed as long as she could, tucking in Alice and Abel and Pretty and checking on Violet in her cheery room on the third floor.

Finally she went to the master bedroom. She turned the lamp low and slipped into her nightgown, for once pulling off her *kapp* and feeling the short curls growing on her head.

Seth had still not come to bed. Right after dinner a mare had started to foal, and both Jacob and Seth had to be with her. Grace kept the light burning so that he would be able to see when he came in the room. She dozed fitfully. Finally, close to midnight, he came in, tired and disheveled.

"Did it go well?" Grace asked.

"Yep, we got a fine little filly. She got up on her legs—long, wobbly legs. I love to see that." He pulled down his suspenders and slipped off his shirt. "I love feeling connected to that first time when the baby rises off the ground and takes its first steps."

Grace was quiet for a moment. "I remember Abel taking his first steps."

Seth looked at her and dropped onto the bed, turning on his side and leaning up on one elbow. "Grace, I was serious today about the adoption. Can we go tomorrow into Lockport?"

"It's Saturday," she reminded him. "The courthouse will be closed."

"All right, then how about Monday next week? I'll tell Jacob I need to take the morning off and we'll go together."

She glanced over at his well-muscled chest and watched the play of breath through his body as his rib cage moved in and out. She thought about the fragility of life and how quickly people could be lost, and she realized that she did not want to lose Seth Wyse.

As if reading her thoughts, he smiled. "Maybe we should talk some—get to know each other better."

"You're tired."

"I'd have to be dead not to want to talk with you. Will you tell me why you never had any more children?"

The question was so casually put that she felt disarmed. "Are you asking me if I'm going to be able to give you children, Seth? We haven't even gotten past kissing, let alone *kinner*."

He laughed, but she didn't miss the seriousness in the depths of his blue eyes. She sighed. "After I conceived Abel, Silas never touched me again in that way. He said my body was a temptation to him and that I was cursed in my appearance."

Seth nodded. "So Abel was born. Was there trouble at the birth? You told me once that he had a brain injury."

Grace fought back tears for a moment. She spoke low and fast and told him how Silas pushed her down a flight of stairs, simply because she hadn't made the corners of the bed square off properly. How terrified she was, and how she didn't tell the doctor the truth when Silas said she had slipped and fallen.

Then she drew a deep breath. "The doctor said that Abel was probably going to be different—he had a swelling on the side of his head when he was born. When he was six months old, I thought he was deaf. He didn't speak, and when he did, it was a muffled kind of sound as if he were speaking underwater. Silas thought of him as inferior, and of course, Abel looked so much like me that Silas also believed he was, well, evil . . ." She trailed off lamely, feeling utterly drained. She had told that story to no one before and it was like lancing an infection from an old wound; she hurt but felt relieved at the same time.

"I am so sorry," Seth said. "Why did you marry him, Grace?"

"I had to marry him to save my family. I couldn't worry about saving myself."

Seth looked at his wife as she lay next to him. He couldn't fathom the pain she had been through, but he was fairly certain he had only gotten a glimpse of it. He didn't know if he'd ever hear the whole story.

But he did know that the Lord gave back. That God was capable of restoring the lost years, capable of healing the pain. And he knew that he was part of that giving back to Grace.

He was determined to be part of it.

"Grace," he whispered, "I want to help make your life better. To give you joy and peace. It doesn't matter to me if we never have another child. I want you to be healed."

"I know. I believe that of you." Her lips quivered as she managed a faint smile. "But I don't know how to do that—to be healed."

"You can't heal yourself," he said. "Only *der Herr* can do that. And I have to tell you the truth, Grace. So long as you let him, Silas Beiler is going to be a ghost between us—a ghost that I can't fight."

She began to cry, and Seth moved closer to gather her in his arms. "Please don't cry, sweetheart. That's not what I want."

She looked up at him, her violet eyes flooding with tears. "Don't tell me that everything will be fine if I just let Silas go. You don't understand. You're perfect, whole; I am flawed and damaged."

He moved closer to stroke her hair. "Grace, I dreamed of you the night before our wedding. I slept under a quilt called Bachelor's Choice. The legend is that when a man sleeps under it, he'll dream of the woman he's to marry. And I dreamed of an Amish woman with pansy-colored eyes, porcelain skin, and black silky hair that was short, so short. That confused me, but in that dream, as I tried to hold you, something sinister rose up from the ground and came between us."

He moved his hand to her shoulder and then to cover her heart. "I know you are troubled inside. Let me help. Please."

Without warning she slipped an arm up behind his back and pressed her mouth against his.

Seth Wyse had kissed any number of girls, but this wasn't like any of them. It was a simple kiss, just her mouth against his, and it was one of the most intimate things he'd ever encountered in his life. Colors flashed behind his eyes, golden-hued starbursts and green, fertile valleys. He had difficulty focusing from the sheer, stilled exuberance he felt.

Maybe *Gott* was teaching him a lesson. Because, for the first time in his life, he experienced the true wonder of a kiss.

CHAPTER 28

Alice lay awake while both Abel and Pretty snored beside her. The furry body next to her stretched and shifted, and she gained comfort from the pup's nearness.

Maybe she should get a dog. They'd never had one; Bud had been allergic.

The thought jarred her awareness: she was a widow now. Single. Alone. Not for the first time, she felt like an alien. What did she think she was doing? Here she was, in a bed in a farmhouse in the middle of Pennsylvania Amish country, instead of in the home that Bud and she had built over all their blessed years together.

But that house held only emptiness—Bud's watch, his glasses, his Bible. His things, his spirit, his memory. But not him.

Everything had happened so fast. The diagnosis of pancreatic cancer, a few months of treatment. And then he was gone.

The morning he died she had gotten him breakfast; he'd eaten a little, then she'd wheeled him back to the home hospice bed where he spent most of his time. Suddenly he couldn't breathe. She had tried not to panic.

She turned up the oxygen to its full five liters, called an ambulance, and listened while Bud breathlessly fussed at her for it. She tried to give him some morphine to relax him, but by the time the ambulance got there, it was too late.

She'd been allowed to ride in the ambulance, but before they could get to the hospital, the love of her life had turned ashen and gasped uselessly like a fish on dry land. A ghastly, wide-mouthed, gaping caricature of all she had known and loved.

The doctor had said that he was in agonal heart rhythm but was no longer breathing. Alice had kissed his still-warm cheek and said good-bye. She couldn't bear to stay when she knew he was gone. She went outside to wait for her sister to come get her, and sat on a bench outside the ER as it thundered and poured rain.

As if the earth itself shared her mourning.

She curved closer to the dog and tried not to think anymore. But she couldn't bring herself to pray.

Grace knew she was dreaming but was caught in the horror of the moment and could not make herself wake. She was trapped beneath the ice with Silas; she saw his body, foreign and familiar, blue and gone. She tried to come up through the same hole into which she had fallen, but she could find no escape. She wanted to cry out, but icy water filled her throat. She was suffocating, collapsing, dying. She sat straight up in bed and screamed.

Seth was beside her, holding her. "What's the matter,

sweetheart? A bad dream? Tell me about it," he urged softly.

"I—I was with Silas, under the ice, under the water. He wanted me to be dead too."

"It's over now. You're with me, and I want you to be alive and happy." She could feel his chin on the top of her head, and then she listened in wonder as he began to pray for her out loud.

"Dear Lord, thank You so much that You have ordained things so that Grace is my wife. Comfort her, free her from the past, and help her to remember that You love her. Help her to know how beautiful she is on the inside. Painter, Father, take the past and reframe it into something beautiful, bright with new color. In Your Son's name, I pray."

Grace felt him draw away from her and she missed the comfort of his touch. She found herself longing to turn to him, to kiss him as she had done the night before, but she resisted.

It was almost dawn. The grace of the prayer still lingering in her ears, she would get up and begin the new day with the new blessing.

Tobias Beiler grabbed his pen and journal and lay down on the small bed. He had already been up, milking and feeding the cows, even though it still wasn't light. He was unused to such manual labor; it didn't suit him at all. Still, the rewards of being so close to Grace far outweighed any pain he felt.

He began to write:

My dearest bruder, Silas, how unfortunate that
you can no longer enjoy the pleasures of your wife. I
have crept close enough to the Wyse farm to see her
at her chores. It comes to me, through a vision of the
Lord, that there must be some way to rid the delightful Grace of her burdensome younger husband. Surely
such a young man cannot manage the headstrong,
sinfully beautiful woman that she is. And as you are
caught beneath the ice, I will take the place that you
can no longer fill . . .

He jumped at the sound of a knock on the door and
thrust the journal beneath his mattress. *"Jah?"*

"Be you well, Abraham?" Mr. Zook's voice came,
faintly concerned but also irritated. "There is work in
the fields."

Tobias flung the door open and smiled. "Simply looking for a pair of gloves. I'll come now."

CHAPTER 29

Seth came in from putting up the horses, tired and dirty. He and Grace were scheduled to go to Jacob and Lilly's for dinner. He wished it might be another night, but it was a good opportunity to get out with Grace. He greeted Abel, who was playing with marbles on the floor, and smiled at Alice. Violet was nowhere about. Grace was washing cups at the sink.

"You look pretty," he said

"Thank you," she murmured. "You look dirty. You'd better hurry."

"Yes, ma'am," Seth said. "It'll only take me a minute."

"I could bring you some clean towels."

"Offering to assist me in my bath?" he asked.

Grace shook her head at his foolery and gave a warning glance over her shoulder at Alice.

"Well, bring them in then, if you please." He headed up to their room and within a minute or two heard her stumping up the stairs on her cast.

"Your towels," Grace said when he opened the door.

"Would you like to come in for a minute?" he asked.

Her eyes strayed to his chest. "We'll be late."

"Sometimes being late is worth it. Do you know how

many family dinners Jacob and Lilly have arrived to flushed and late over the past months?"

She shook her head. He smiled and closed the door softly behind them.

Her heart fluttered like an excited bird as she gazed up into his deep blue eyes. She said the first thing that came to mind.

"You look tired."

"I am."

"*Ach*, then maybe we should wait until—"

"Until what, Grace?" He reached to take the towels from her and tossed them on the bed.

She wet her lips. "I—I don't know." A thought crossed her mind abruptly. "Have—have you kissed other girls before?"

He turned his eyes away.

"Have you?"

"Yes," he admitted.

She spun from him and sat down on the edge of the bed, her knees together, her hands clenched in her lap and her chin tilted upward. "I want to know."

He moved to kneel at her feet. "What do you want to know? And why?"

She forced herself to answer. "Because you know about my . . . past. I want to know about yours."

He took her hand and laid it over his heart, pressing her fingers to his skin.

"Grace, you alone hold my heart and always will."

"I would know," she insisted.

He smiled and let her go, sinking back on his legs to put his hands on his thighs. He looked up at her.

"Sweet, sweet Grace, very well. There was my first kiss—"

"How old were you?" she snapped, surprised at the prick of jealousy she felt at his honest words.

"Fifteen . . . Her name was Ada, an *Englisch* girl, visiting the *Amisch* country from Ireland. She tasted of fresh mint and clover and—" He half closed his eyes.

"All right," Grace cut him off. "I get Ada. Who else?"

He tilted his head, considering. "Mary and Martha. They were twins, not very charitable to one another but especially indulgent where I was concerned."

Grace huffed with displeasure. *Maybe this wasn't such a good idea.*

"Ellen was *Englisch* too. Her *daed* had a big house. He was never home—"

"All right, Seth Wyse!" She slapped her palms on her knees and stood up, hobbling past him.

"What? You asked." He stared at her innocently.

She ground her teeth in frustration and whirled to go out the door, trying to ignore the sound of his soft laughter behind her.

When she gained the hall, she pressed her back against the wall, attempting to compose herself. But the words she'd demanded of him echoed in her head and she feared that she would never be good enough to match the memories that burned in his brain.

Seth lifted one of the cotton towels from the bed and went to splash water on his chest and arms. He knew enough about women to know she was jealous.

Which meant she cared.

At least a bit.

CHAPTER 30

The evening had cooled, and fireflies had begun to make their appearance. Against his will and common sense, Luke King decided to drive over to the Wyse farm.

His older brother James stood at the barn door blocking his way. "Where are you going at this hour?"

Luke scowled. "Out."

"Out why?"

"James, come on, let me by. I need—well, I need to talk to Seth Wyse about Lacy's lameness. Wondered if he could do something to help."

James laughed. "Why not ask Grant? He's a vet."

"Seth knows about as much." Luke hitched up the buggy and mounted the seat.

"And he houses a cure for what ails you." James laughed again.

"Forget it. Just move."

James stepped aside with a graceful bow. "Of course. Happy courting."

Luke glared at him. "I am not—"

But his *bruder* had already turned back to the barn. Luke grasped the reins with one hand and swiped at his hair with the other. Even if it was a fool's errand over a meddlesome and provoking girl, he'd look half decent doing it.

The summer twilight blanketed the buggy in soft darkness as Seth, Grace, and Abel drove the short distance to Lilly and Jacob's house. Abel was mesmerized by the hundreds of lightning bugs out in the fields, blinking like a silent symphony, a chorus of soothing wonder.

Alice had elected to stay home and study her Pink Lady sales brochures, and Grace had convinced Abel to let Pretty stay home as company for Alice. Violet, distracted and dreamy, had also declined.

Jacob answered the door wearing his best green shirt, and suddenly it felt like a party atmosphere. "Come in," he said. "Lilly's *mamm* is at her support group tonight, so we are alone."

Seth watched Grace talking to Lilly and hoped that the two would become even better friends. Maybe Grace would open up some with his *bruder's* wife.

As he hugged Lilly in greeting, he felt the slight curve to her stomach and laughed out loud. "I forgot in the whole marriage business that I am soon to be an *onkel*!"

Everyone laughed, then Abel spoke up. "Who's *my* uncle?" he asked. "Nooooot Uncle Tobias?" The boy began to frown.

"*Nee*," Seth said calmly. "Your uncle is Jacob."

Abel's face lit up. "I have a *gut* uncle, an uncle, an uncle . . ." He played out loud with the word as if testing the sound for its value and meaning.

"What is that delicious smell?" Grace asked.

"Well, I have to confess." Lilly smiled. "I'm cooking Indian food. Curried chicken with apples and avocado. Since I've gotten pregnant, I've been craving spicy foods. I found this recipe in a cookbook in Lockport, and Jacob will eat whatever I give him. I hope you all like it."

Seth found the meal a bit odd, but delicious. They finished with a carrot cake with cream cheese frosting, and Abel ate two slices. The boy obviously preferred sweets to salty foods, yet he was lean as a willow switch.

During coffee, Jacob asked, "How are things going with you two?"

Seth reached down and petted Love, the dog. He avoided looking at Grace.

"Fine," Grace answered. "We're doing very well."

Seth tried to take this as a good sign. After all, Jacob and Lilly had struggles in the beginning, but somehow the Lord had helped them work through them. He hoped God would do the same for him and Grace.

Finally Jacob rose from the table. "It's time for chores. Let's leave the womenfolk alone. Abel, do you want to come with us and help?"

Abel looked at his *mamm* in faint alarm. She touched his shoulder lightly. "It's okay if you'd like to stay here and do some coloring books or play with something that Lilly has around."

Abel nodded, and a light went on in Seth's head. What was the difference, he wondered, between coloring books and painting? He'd have a conversation with Grace about that issue later.

He put on his hat and followed Jacob out to the barn.

"Well, how *is* it going?" Jacob asked once they'd begun to rotate feed among the stock.

Seth shrugged. "I think I made her jealous tonight, before we came."

"What did you do now?"

"She asked me about my past—with girls, you know. I told her a little."

"Are you out of your mind? You *never* tell a woman about other women. Even I know that."

"What about you and Sarah?"

"There was no me and Sarah—only in my imagination. But you—you've kissed more girls than I care to count." He shook a long finger in Seth's face. "You *never* kiss and tell. What is wrong with you?"

Seth sighed. "I'm desperate, I guess. Do you know what it is to have the woman of your dreams within arm's reach and find her cool as alabaster? A snow maiden, trapped by her own past." He looked at his brother seriously. "Can you give me some more advice, Jacob, about when you were first married? I know there were problems, but with Grace it seems so difficult— she is so distant."

"You need to take time to learn little things about her. I mean, you know she quilts, and she's probably terrified of honeybees now, but what else? What really makes her tick?"

Seth thought hard. "I don't know."

"That's what I mean—you need to get to know your wife. Believe me, I did a lot of time praying in this barn, and to tell the truth, a lot of bawling, when Lilly and I were first married."

Seth thought on his *bruder's* words and did not know how to respond. He looked around at the warm barn as if it might hold an answer. The smell of the hay drifted on the summer night air.

Jacob studied him and Seth tried to avoid his brother's eyes, but Jacob was persistent. "What happened after the bees? Did she talk to you at all?"

"No, not really. She actually found my painting room and discovered a painting that I had been working on of her and Abel."

"Oh boy."

"She was not happy. I told her that it was not the way I wanted to paint her, though."

"How do you want to paint her?" Jacob arched an eyebrow.

"I want to paint her as she is to me—a deep pond with vibrant colors around it. A pond with rocks, so the stream that trickles into it can make music. A pond with trees that burgeon with color, and ripe with fish and turtles and frogs and—"

"You want to paint her like a frog?"

"No, of course not." Not for the first time, Seth found himself frustrated with his brother's concrete way of thinking. "You can't understand. I'm trying to get at the hidden reserves of strength that I see in her. She's so much more than just a beautiful woman, Jacob."

"Well, I told you that," his brother said with a laugh. "And it sounds like you're growing up a bit, Seth Wyse."

"Yeah, but in a lot of ways, it's like she's still a stranger. I hate to say it, but I think I know Abel better than his mother."

"She is not a stranger. Come on. You can make a difference with her, I know you can. And I know it sounds *narrisch*, but once you discover that closeness, you can change the world. Seth, look at what happened with Lilly's mom—we were able to help her and save her life."

"How is Lilly's *mamm*, anyway?"

"Well, tonight she's off to her support group, and we make sure she keeps up with her meds. She's doing very well, actually."

"I'm glad," Seth said. "I'm really glad. Do you think she will eventually move out on her own to the *daudi haus*?"

Jacob shrugged. "When the *kinner* start to come, maybe."

Seth laughed. "And they're coming! So tell me the answer to the eternal question—do you want a boy or a girl? And no fair citing 'just healthy' either."

Jacob ducked his head. "Truth be told—and don't repeat it—I'd like a little girl, with Lilly's brown hair and blue eyes. I want to see the Lilly I missed when we were in school together."

"Yeah, you noticed nothing but Sarah then."

"Right. But I was wrong, and God turned it around. God can turn this around for you too. You've got to have faith, Seth."

He nodded slowly. "Well, that's the trick, isn't it?"

CHAPTER 31

Violet sat idly on the front steps of the house, warm kerosene light burning gently in the windows behind her. She felt particularly dreamy that evening, turning over in her mind the brief encounters she'd had with Luke King. The *Englisch* spoke of "love at first sight," and she wondered if it was true for some people. The problem was getting Luke to believe it.

She looked up in surprise as a rapidly moving horse and buggy swung into the circle in front of the house. Then she recognized Luke, and her heart began to pound. A materialization of her dreams, maybe even a confirmation from *der Herr* about her feelings.

She smoothed her apron, then rose to greet him. His hair was slicked down, and he wore a clean white shirt. He slipped his hat off in deference to her.

"Hello, Mr. King," she said. "Is there something that you need?"

She watched as his Adam's apple bobbed for a minute. "Look, Violet, I came . . . I came to tell you to let me be. I'm not the marrying kind. I do what I want to do in life."

"Like saving baby caterpillars?" She took a step toward

him and he backed off. "Why don't we go for a ride? It's such a beautiful night."

His jaw muscle twitched. "Did you hear what I said?"

She turned back to the house. "Alice!" she called through the screen door. "I'm going for a buggy ride with Luke King."

Alice appeared briefly in the doorway. "Fine with me. Have fun."

Violet scampered up into the buggy and looked down at Luke with innocent eyes. "I think we can discuss your concerns better if you're driving."

He muttered darkly under his breath, slapped his hat against his thigh, then mounted the seat beside her.

"You," he said, "are not . . . are not . . ."

"I know," she said. "Let's go."

After Violet left, Alice tried to concentrate on learning the benefits of a particular Pink Lady night cream, but the familiar fear ate at her again. She hated being alone, even though the dog was with her. She tried to cling to her faith, remembering that God had promised to protect her. But she still felt her heart pound and closed the brochure to pace the kitchen.

Then Pretty began to seem antsy.

"Oh great," Alice moaned. "You need to go out, right?"

The pup seemed to nod her assent and whirled around, pounding her tail on the hardwood floor.

Alice sighed and picked up the kerosene lamp from the kitchen table. "All right. Lord, protect an old woman from her silly fears."

She went to the door and had barely pushed open the screen when Pretty dashed through and ran out like a streak into the night. This was no bathroom call; the dog was growling and barking in the distance.

"Oh boy," Alice muttered, stepping off the porch. "Probably she's seen a cat. Pretty! Here, Pretty!"

She called in vain for a while and then stood in indecision, her gaze drifting to the backdrop of stars against the frame of the mountains. Bud used to say, "A person can't know God as Redeemer if they don't first know Him as Creator." And who was it that made the mountains and flung the stars into space? The same God who loved and looked out for her.

Just as she was uttering a prayer of thanks, Pretty rushed to her out of the dark.

"At last!" Alice exclaimed. She shooed the dog up the steps. "I hope you didn't bother a cat, you silly dog."

Then she closed the door on the night with a sigh of relief.

"Have you ever kissed a girl?" Violet framed the question in the same carefree tone she might use if she were asking about the weather. His long hands tightened on the reins.

"It's none of your business."

"Surely it is." She laid her hand on his arm and felt the heavy muscles tense beneath her fingertips.

"I don't even know what I'm doing with you."

"We're building our future, of course," Violet replied. "*Ach*, look! A shooting star. Quick! Make a wish."

She felt him shift beside her. "I wish I understood women."

She patted his arm and stifled a laugh. "Now, that wish, Mr. King, is not about to come true."

Abel sat on the floor quietly coloring while Grace and Lilly sat at the table drinking tea. Grace had spent time with Lilly before, but for some reason, she now felt uncomfortable. Lilly must have sensed it because she reached across the table and caught Grace's hand.

"Is there anything wrong, Grace?"

"What has Jacob told you about . . . about us?" Grace asked, unconsciously fingering a spot on her neck where a bee sting still left a red welt.

Lilly pulled her hand away and stirred her tea. "He told me about the bees, and—well, he told me Seth was pretty upset yesterday for some reason. He wouldn't go into detail. Those two are very private and are best friends. They share so much together."

"Yes," Grace said. "I suppose I should become the one who is sharing with Seth, at least a little—it's not an easy process, though."

"I know firsthand that you cannot become best friends overnight when you marry someone you barely know. I had spent a lifetime fantasizing about Jacob, but I didn't really know him, or how deep his heart was, or how much fun he was, or how considerate."

"You really are in love, aren't you?"

"*Jah.*" Lilly's blue eyes grew bright. "And what about you, Grace?" The question hung in the air between the two women, and when Grace did not reply, she heard Lilly draw a deep breath. "Will you tell me please about your first husband? What was he like—Abel's father?"

Grace bowed her head. "I wish I could explain it. I wish I could say anything good, in fact. I guess the best thing I can say is that he was Abel's father and, without him, I wouldn't have my son. But as for being in love, I don't even know what that means. I don't even know what it feels like."

"Give Seth a chance," Lilly said. "Ever since he laid eyes on you, his artist's eyes, there has been no one else."

"There are other younger women about," Grace said. "I am, after all, so much older than him."

Lilly laughed. "You are not. You're beautiful, and honestly, when I first met you, I couldn't tell how old you were. I thought maybe you were as young as nineteen, but your eyes—your eyes are wise and sad. Won't you please share some of that sadness with me so that I can help you?"

"You've helped me already, simply by talking, by accepting me," Grace said. "But yes, someday I'll tell you my story. I think I owe it to Seth to tell him first. I owe it to him to let him know exactly what kind of person I am."

Grace paused and looked up as the men came in the door. Soon they all sat together, laughing and talking, and then it was time to go home. Abel did not want to go, and he started to fuss. Grace was embarrassed, but fortunately Lilly diverted him by allowing him to take the coloring book with him and a few of the crayons.

"Since school is out for the summer," Lilly said in

her sternest teacher voice, "you should be doing something productive with your time."

Abel agreed.

On the ride home, the mountain road was inky dark. The trees were giant shadows; the grassy roadsides filled with the fragrance of flowers. The mountains enclosed them like an embrace as they drove along.

"Did you have a good time?" Seth asked.

Grace nodded as she held a drowsing Abel against her side. He was near asleep in a matter of minutes.

It was a characteristic of his autism: social situations, which to others seemed fun, could be stressful for him, and afterward he would simply shut down. Sometimes Grace wished she had that ability as well—to turn off, to shut down. Mostly she wished she could understand the inner workings of her son's mind better; what went on inside his brain, how much he remembered of his father. She hoped it wasn't a great deal.

Seth reached over and covered her hand with his. She felt the strong bones, warm palm, and calm confidence of him, and she sensed an answering response from deep in her heart. Maybe tonight he might kiss her again. The thought went through her—unbidden, uncalled for, but still present.

Yet he didn't seem prepared to make such a move. Alice took a drowsy Abel and Pretty off to bed, and then Grace and Seth went through the act of climbing into bed in the darkness. Seth removed his shirt and lay down with his trousers still on. Grace waited until the light was doused to change into her nightgown.

Grace slipped into bed and took a few deep breaths

before she spoke. "Lilly and Jacob seem to be very much in love."

She heard him move beneath the sheets and then he sighed faintly. "They are, but it was a long road to get there."

"I'm sorry about earlier today—pressing you about the past when you've been so gentle with asking about my own," she said.

"I'm sorry for telling. I should have had the sense to keep my mouth shut, I guess."

"No," she protested quietly. "You are—were—you are what you are. I just think that I won't ever be able to match up to those girls. All those girls."

He let out a little bark of a laugh and reached out to clasp her shoulder. "Grace, I can't explain it, but I feel like I've been waiting for you all my life. Those girls don't matter—any more than Silas Beiler matters."

She shivered at his touch, but her words were mournful. "It seems that Silas will always matter."

She felt his hand slip away, and soon his even breathing told her that he was deeply asleep. She slid out from beneath the light quilt in the darkness and came around the bed. With sure fingers, she felt on the dresser, found the matches, and lit a candle.

Carrying its mellow light before her in the surrounding darkness, she slid the candleholder onto Seth's bedside table. She smiled down at him. He was deeply asleep, his golden hair tousled against the pillow. It was like coming close to some strong, wild animal, lazing in the sun, yet having the instinctive knowledge that there was safety there too.

She trailed one finger lightly down his cheek.

He stirred, but he did not wake.

He was dreaming, the deep, involved kind of dream that teases the senses and blurs the boundary between reality and imagination. He was lying in an apple orchard in spring; the fragrant white blossoms contrasted with the deep blue sky above. He lay on his back, one arm behind his head, his knees bent as he looked up into Grace's smiling face. He had a sketch pad in his lap, balanced against his knees. He wanted her to bend closer so that he could steal a kiss and make the picture complete in his mind. But she'd gotten hold of a small brush and was touching his face with it. He was afraid if he moved, she'd stop, so he held himself purposefully still.

She trailed the brush down one shoulder, then traced the length of one arm and up the other, swirling the delicate bristles across his wrist and hand and then across the breadth of his chest.

Seth sat up in the darkness and tried to slow his breathing. The faint smell of candle smoke tickled his nose, and he peered over in the bed, trying to make out the outline of Grace's form beneath the sheets. He touched her once, a grazing brush of his knuckles along her hip, but she didn't move.

He flung an arm over his eyes and tried to go back to sleep.

But the dream was much too vivid, and the scent of the candle too strong.

CHAPTER 32

Tobias was growing used to the hard work of being a hired man. He'd managed to balance his time shrewdly with enough work to allow him time to slip off through the fields and spy on the Wyse place. After last night's visit, he decided that the kid's dog was a hindrance and he had to do something about her. But the thought gave him no satisfaction; he had an affection for animals and couldn't see himself lifting a hand to an innocent creature.

He entered the kitchen for breakfast and sat down at the table among the various-aged children. "A fair morning to you," he said to *Fraa* Zook.

Deacon Zook already had his seat and asked his wife as to the whereabouts of Kate, their eldest daughter.

Tobias said nothing, though he might have predicted that the chit was still in bed. Seventeen-year-old Kate Zook was too intent and too aware of her own beauty. Compared to Grace, who reminded him of a dewy violet, she was an ostentatious iris.

The girl finally arrived and gave Tobias a haughty, condescending glance. He looked down at his plate and waited until silent grace was finished before helping himself to the bacon.

"So, Abraham, my husband tells me that you come from Ohio originally," Esther Zook began in a conversational tone. From listening to her at mealtimes, Tobias already knew her to be a venomous gossip. It might not hurt to let slip a few tidbits about Grace—just enough for the community to begin to question her integrity.

"Jah . . . Middle Hollow or thereabouts," he murmured.

"Middle Hollow?" Esther Zook straightened in her chair like a spring gobbler. "Why, our neighbor, the newly married Grace Wyse, comes from there. Did you know her? Her last name was Beiler."

Tobias shrugged. "I've heard the name Beiler. There were several Amish communities thereabout, but the one Beiler fella was said to be a rich man." He reached for another biscuit.

Esther leaned in over her plate. "I heard her husband met an unfortunate end."

He nodded. "Did hear something like that."

"Well, Grace Beiler was awful high-handed when she came here, sticking to herself and her son. The boy's got some sort of mental problem. Anyway, she up and married one of our neighbor boys—someone I'd hoped that our Kate here might—"

"Esther." Deacon Zook raised a hand. "I want to enjoy my breakfast. Let's speak of other things."

Tobias watched Esther Zook bristle and then fall silent. She might obey her husband in the moment, but she couldn't change her nature. Once a gossip, always a gossip.

Seth was glad when the first light of dawn stretched across the expanse of the window. He swung out of bed and was pulling on a blue shirt when his wife slowly awoke and sat up. She rubbed at her eyes like a little girl and he turned away as he tucked in his shirt.

He needed a diversion—a safe diversion—after his fruitless night's sleep. "Hey," he said, turning back to her. "Why don't we do something fun today? Let's take Alice to town. She can see all the Amish stuff, the souvenir things, and then we can go to lunch, and you and Violet can do some shopping. You haven't gone shopping in weeks. I know you must need things for the house."

She hesitated. "I don't know, Seth. I . . . well, I haven't yet been paid in full for the wedding quilt."

Seth had never spoken with Grace about finances. She had no true idea how much property the Wyse family had been blessed with, or how well off they were.

He supposed there was no time like the present.

Grace watched as Seth sat down on the edge of the bed and turned to her. She sensed a serious conversation coming on. "I know it's not always something that's comfortable to talk about, but we might as well discuss finances as long as the subject has come up." He reached out to stroke her hand where it lay against the quilt.

Money, in Grace's experience, had always produced stress. She desperately wanted to avoid an argument if possible, and she wished she'd never said anything about it. "Uh, we really don't have to discuss it. Just tell me how much I have to spend and how you want it spent, and I'll make it work."

"Grace," he said softly. "You told me that you married Silas Beiler to save your family. Did it have something to do with money?"

She slid her hand from his and curled up with her arms around her knees. "*Jah*. My family was bad off in debt. If . . . if I married Silas, he would take care of all of that and buy my mother's medicines. It seemed I had no choice at the time."

"Didn't the community step in to help?"

"One too many times, as far as the bishop was concerned, I guess. And then—well, Silas was wealthy, but I couldn't buy so much as a piece of fabric without his approval. So I'd really rather you handled all of this and we not talk about it," she finished in a rush.

"Sweetheart, we have to talk about it. First of all, the Wyse family holdings and the horse-breeding farm are extensive in their earnings and worth." He named a sum that made her eyebrows shoot up; it was nearly triple of what she knew to be Silas's assets.

"I—I don't know what to say. I certainly didn't marry you for your money."

He laughed out loud and slid closer to her on the bed. "Of course you didn't, but what I have is yours. And there's also what *Daed* calls the old money— wealth dating back hundreds of years, which has more or less accrued as time has gone on." Again he shocked her with the amount.

"So . . . you're rich?"

"*Jah*, but so are you. And I'd be exactly as rich with not so much as a penny to my name, so long as I had you and Abel."

She looked into his eyes and knew what he said to be true.

"Grace, the Lord has chosen to bless us. You need never worry about money or my approval for something that you buy. Buy anything you need for you, Abel, the house. I'll tend to the outdoor purchases, and we can talk together about investments. How does that sound?"

"Fine," she said, still cautious.

"*Gut!*" He brushed a quick kiss against her temple, then bounced off the bed and went to the bureau they shared. He withdrew an envelope from one of the top drawers and handed it to her. "Here, use this until I get your checkbook set up, okay? And tell me if you need more."

Grace peered inside the envelope. Without counting, she knew it was more than Silas had given her to spend in all the years of their marriage combined. She looked up at Seth.

"*Danki*," she said with seriousness.

He smiled at her again. "You are more than welcome."

CHAPTER 33

Seth hitched up his suspenders, pleased that he was able to provide well for his wife and *sohn*, but knowing that it was only through the Lord's grace. "We'll go Monday to the courthouse to start the adoption process," he said. "Today we can simply have some fun."

"Won't Jacob ask about you taking off on Monday?" she asked.

"Jacob won't say anything. Do you know how many days he's taken off to help Lilly around the farm or to take Lilly or her mother to an appointment?" He arched one eyebrow. "Although I'm pretty sure I know what some of those *appointments* were about." Grace giggled; it was a delightful sound, like a clear bell ringing.

He whistled softly as he left Grace to dress and went downstairs to start breakfast. When he got to the kitchen, Alice was already busy at the stove.

"How did you sleep?" she asked, giving him a wink.

"Just fine. How are you doing, sleeping with Abel and Pretty?"

"I think Abel would like to be a bedmate of mine for some time. We talked about it this morning."

"Miss Alice tells me stories," Abel piped up from the table.

"That's great." Seth ruffled the boy's hair with a gentle hand.

But given his restlessness last night, he wasn't sure lingering nights with Grace were a blessing or a curse. He sat down to scrambled eggs, bacon, and grilled tomatoes and was just beginning to eat when Grace joined them quietly.

She wore a dark blue blouse under a black dress. Grace dressed to hide herself and her beauty. He'd have to do something about that. Maybe he'd buy her violet fabric, he thought suddenly—a color that would match her eyes.

He talked to Abel and Alice as he ate, and then announced their trip to town. Jacob came in the door at that moment for a cup of coffee.

"Just stopped by to touch base on that new foal," Jacob said. He stopped and looked at Alice.

"Jacob." Seth waved a hand. "Meet Alice Miller . . . Grace's *Englisch* friend."

"Hiya," Jacob said, extending a hand.

Alice smiled. "Where do grown men like you folks come from? I swear handsome men seem to rise from the ground wherever I look. But you're far too young for me, and I bet you have a wife anyway."

Jacob smiled politely at Alice's ramblings, then sat down at the table.

Alice poured him a big cup of coffee.

"Jacob, we're going to town today. We've got an appointment with fun, and I'm going to have another appointment on Monday," Seth said casually.

Jacob raised an amused eyebrow. "Really, now?"

"*Jah*," Grace said quickly. "On Monday we're going to the courthouse. I haven't had a chance to talk to Abel, but maybe now is a good time."

Abel looked up. "Talk to me about what?"

Grace felt many pairs of eyes stare at her. She could, of course, take Abel outside to have the conversation with him; he might say something that would hurt Seth. But on the other hand, maybe this was the better way.

"Abel," she said seriously, moving closer to him on the bench. "Seth has asked if he could adopt you."

"Adopt me? But I belong to you." The boy's pale brow puckered with worry.

"Adopting you would mean that you would have the same last name as I do—Wyse."

"My last name is Beiler."

Grace bit her lip. "Abel, that's right, but since your father died, you could be Abel Wyse now."

"Abel Wyse, Abel Wyse . . . ," the boy sing-songed, trying it out on his tongue. He shook his head, then looked down at his eggs. "Okay, I like it."

Grace breathed a silent sigh of relief, then Abel looked back up again in Seth's direction.

"Can you adopt Pretty too, Seth?"

"You betcha."

Abel went back to his eggs, but he hummed a little and sang to himself, "Pretty Wyse, Pretty Wyse."

Grace sought to change the subject. "Jacob, how is Lilly feeling?"

"Right as rain and growing rounder by the day. The midwife says she's doing well. You go and have fun in town. My brother's done my work for me on more than one occasion. But don't be too late—there's supposed to be a storm tonight. I heard it from old Deacon Zook, and he's always right about the weather."

Jacob drained his coffee cup and put it in the sink, then waved good-bye and left. Alice came to the table. "We're taking a special trip to town? Let me go get my pocketbook."

"Let it be my treat," Seth said. "I'll treat the ladies and the young gentleman to a day in town."

Going to town was not something Grace did very often before she married Seth. She had seen no real reason to go—mostly she felt like avoiding people, truth be told, and had probably been a little bit depressed.

But the prospect of town with her husband, *sohn*, and good friend seemed more than fitting, and there was a skip in her step as she went out to the buggy.

They all crowded in together, she and Seth in the front, Alice and Violet in the back, and Abel sitting on a small stool in the front between them. Seth made the ride merry with stories and jokes that had even Abel smiling. For the first time in a very long while, Grace felt a thrill of joy go through her.

Tobias crept through the tall corn until he reached the border of the Wyse farm. He'd seen Grace drive off earlier with her pretty-boy husband, the kid, the sister, and some other woman. None of the older folks were around. It was the perfect opportunity to make the first move in his mission.

The plan was pretty simple. Grace was fragile enough that it wouldn't take much to terrify her. With the right kind of threat to her son, or her sister, or even the new husband, he could drive her out of Pine Creek and straight into his net. Once before, with Silas, she had sacrificed herself for the sake of her family. She'd do it again. And then Tobias would have it all: the farm, the inheritance, the woman.

He approached the shaded area where the young dog lay on a comfortable tether. He fed her the remainder of his bacon from breakfast, then bent to rub the soft head. "It's okay, girl," he said quietly. "Everything's fine."

He and Silas had a puppy once when they were young. Their father had drowned it as punishment when Tobias had forgotten to close the barn door.

He pushed away from such memories and turned his attention to the empty house.

CHAPTER 34

Seth navigated the buggy through the small streets of town. The *Englisch* people didn't look up much; they were accustomed to the Amish being about, and many stores had a hitching post next to a parking meter. They passed Emily's Mystery and Seth shot Grace a grin.

"What's the mystery of Emily?" Alice asked from the back of the buggy where she and Violet were crowded together. "It sounds like they might have some exotic things to look at in there."

Grace craned her neck around to look at her friend. "No, Alice, that's actually a shop for . . . women's undergarments." His wife spoke softly and glanced meaningfully at Abel. But it was too late.

"Underwear!" Abel said. He began to repeat the word in different intonations, louder and louder. Seth could not contain his laughter, and soon Grace and Alice and Violet were joining in. Fortunately, Abel settled down as they stopped at the library.

"If it's okay, I think I'll take a walk around town," Violet said.

Grace waved her on with a smile.

"I like going to the library," Alice announced. "Maybe I'll pick me up a good Amish romance to read. Although I hardly need a book. I could just look as far as you two."

Seth shook his head and held open the heavy wooden door for them to enter.

The library was a long, squat white building made of cinder block. It had survived the terrible flood of twenty years before, and the permanent smell of musty books seemed to drift in the air.

"Do you have a card here?" Seth asked Grace.

"*Nee.* I haven't had the chance to visit yet."

"Well, we'll fix that right now."

At the front desk, an owlish *Englisch* woman perched on a swivel chair. She had gray hair, tightly permed, glasses perched on her small nose, and a kind smile.

"I don't think I've met all of you before, although Seth, I know."

"Everyone, this is Viv, librarian extraordinaire." Seth bowed slightly as Grace and Alice shook hands with the other woman. Grace couldn't help but notice that Seth and the librarian were well acquainted. Here was another facet of her husband she did not know: he must love to read.

Abel pulled at her skirt, pointing to an open, light blue room with a carousel of children's books. "Mama, can I go there?"

"*Jah,*" she answered. He scampered off alone.

"I'll set everyone up for a library card," Viv said. "We're sort of old-fashioned here; we only need your name and phone number. But I guess you all won't be having phones, right? Never mind. I know where to find you if a book goes missing!"

She laughed easily and Grace found herself liking the woman, especially when she offered to go help Abel find a book.

Grace drifted down the quiet aisles, feeling the delicious freedom of being alone and untroubled for a moment. Only a few people were in the library at this time of the morning, and she nearly jumped out of her skin when Seth came up behind her as she reached for a book.

"*Fashions of the 1800s*? Is this really what you want?" he teased.

"Well," Grace said, "I know it may be vanity, but I do like to look at skirt patterns."

"Do you now?" He took a step closer. The library row was cool and intimate; the books seemed to speak in whispers of time and love and mystery. She clutched her choice to her chest for a moment, then slid it back onto the shelf.

Alice selected three Amish romances from a shelf near the main desk at the library. "Bet these are popular," she said, smiling at Viv. It was the first time she'd met someone in the community who was *Englisch* and near her own age.

"Oh yes," Viv agreed. "It's easy to explore issues in the simpler setting of those books. That one deals with loss in particular."

Alice nodded and started to return the book to its place on the shelf. Viv must have read the expression on her face. "I'm sorry—I didn't mean to imply that the books are heavy reading. They're actually very inspirational. I guess we can all use a little of that now and then."

"Yes," Alice admitted in a low voice. "That's why I came to visit with Grace—looking for something to take my mind off the usual."

"What is usual in your life?" Viv asked.

Alice looked into Viv's eyes and recognized a kindred spirit. "I lost my husband a few months back," she said. "Took it harder than I thought I would. Actually got to be afraid in my own house." She swallowed hard. "I guess I ran away for a while, but sooner or later I'm going to have to face home again."

Viv touched her arm. "I lost my Ernie two years ago. Felt like I was losing my mind in that big old house. I wanted to die, to be with him in heaven, but I have slowly come to understand that grief is a journey. Once you start out, there's no going back. God makes it that way until our minds and bodies and spirits can adjust to the loss and then go on in His strength. I don't mean to be forward, but you are also seeing love in its earliest beginnings with Seth and his wife. Surely that must be hard on you?"

Alice thought for a moment, then shook her head. "No, it encourages me somehow, reassures me that life goes on." She cleared her throat, then tapped the paperbacks in front of her. "I'll take out these. And . . . thank you, Viv."

Viv stamped the books and smiled. "Anytime you want more company than the books, let me know."

Alice clutched the novels to her and felt in her Pink Lady bag for a brochure. "And anytime you want a free beauty consultation or new eye makeup, let me know." She gripped Viv's hand for a moment, then sniffed.

"I'll go and check on the boy."

"Well, well, what do we have here?"

Grace looked up to see an *Amisch* girl—a beautiful blond *Amisch* girl with green eyes—headed down the aisle toward them. The girl's voice dripped with sarcasm, a distinct and unattractive contrast to the beauty of the young face.

"Kate, good morning," Seth said easily. "Do you know my wife, Grace?"

Grace nodded to the younger girl. She had met Kate Zook at church Meeting but had never had any real personal contact with her.

She watched as the girl laid a proprietary hand on her husband's arm. "Seth, I'm thinking about buying the new mare that I saw running about in your pasture—the palomino."

"Then talk to Jacob. He's handling that horse."

A nervous discomfort flooded through Grace and she turned to leave. But Kate Zook blocked her path. "Running away, *Fraa* Wyse?"

Grace didn't respond. Seth cleared his throat. "Kate," he said in a warning tone. The girl laughed and left them with a lingering look at Seth.

Grace sighed and turned to him. "How old are you?"

"What?"

"I asked you how old you are."

"Why?"

"Because Kate is a young girl and I—I—"

"Twenty-four."

"Oh." She looked up at him with some alarm.

"Disappointed?" There was an edge to his voice.

"No, I—it's only that I'm twenty-seven."

He crossed his arms over his chest and looked at her. "A nice number."

"Seth, I—"

"Look, can we drop the whole age thing? It doesn't matter one bit. There's always going to be someone older or younger. I don't care."

Grace drew in a deep breath, then straightened her spine. "All right. No more age worries, young girls or old."

"Gut!" He laughed out loud, only to be shushed by Viv.

"Tell me one thing, though," she whispered. "Was Kate Zook part of your . . . past?"

"Does it matter?"

"Yes."

"Okay. No. She wasn't. And let's just admit that we've had very different pasts. I was making out in buggies while you were trying to survive."

She nodded. "It's true."

"Well, it's also true that I haven't so much as looked at another woman since we married."

She shrugged. "I haven't looked at another man either." Then she started to laugh at the sheer absurdity of her response.

"Why are you laughing?"

"Because I only look at you."

"Now that, my sweet, I can live with." He reached down and caught her hand. "Come on. We'd better find Alice before she picks all the Amish romances."

She gave him a shy smile. "She could look right here," Grace said, echoing Alice's earlier words.

"So she could, my *fraa*. So she could."

Luke King suppressed a groan when he recognized the voice of Violet Beiler behind him. Did the girl have some sort of sixth sense? Here he was, loading feed bags into the back of a wagon. It was hot, heavy work, and he was soaked with sweat. He tried to concentrate on counting the sacks as he lifted them, but her voice distracted him.

"Hello there, Mr. King."

"Three . . . four . . . five."

"Be polite, now," she said.

He turned. "When are you going to act like a proper girl? I tell you, I don't know what to do with you."

It was true. One minute he wanted to turn her over his knee, and the next minute he wanted to kiss her. Unfortunately, he'd had little experience in either.

She stood there looking at him, saying nothing, her blue eyes wide and innocent. He never thought he understood women, but in that moment, he understood *her*. She wasn't playing games with him. She wasn't being coy. She wasn't flirting.

She genuinely wanted him. This beautiful woman

with the clear blue eyes and dazzling smile wanted him, Luke King, bachelor farmer.

He couldn't help himself. Despite his best intentions, he stepped forward and put his hands on her shoulders. Filthy as he was, sweaty with work and covered with grain dust from the feed sacks, he pulled her close and kissed her.

She didn't move away. Didn't turn up her nose at his smell. Didn't shrink from the dirt.

She kissed him back.

How long they stood there, Luke had no idea. He finally pulled away when he heard the distant sound of a wagon. He stared down at her beautiful face and saw unshed tears in her blue, blue eyes.

He thumbed his dirty hands across her cheeks and exhaled heavily, trying to slow his breathing.

"You . . . you can call me Luke."

And then she smiled.

"So," Grace asked in the sweetest tone she could muster. "Is there anyone else I should be prepared to meet? I mean, there's a girl on the other side of the street . . ."

He glanced across the way. *"Nee,"* he murmured. "I don't know her."

She gave in to the giggle that bubbled from deep inside her and elbowed him hard in the ribs.

"Are you laughing, Grace?" He rubbed his side and peered down at her from beneath the brim of his straw hat.

"*Jah*, I guess I am."

"Well—" He seemed at a loss for once. "I praise the Lord for that."

She laughed again. "Me too."

CHAPTER 35

As they neared home, Grace seemed to be pressed closer to him on the buggy seat than she had been on the way in. Seth was about to remark on this proximity when he looked up to see Jacob riding fast toward them on Thunder, his black gelding. Immediately Seth had a gut feeling that something was wrong, and he started to pray beneath his breath.

Jacob drew up alongside the buggy. His face was angry and flushed.

"What is it?" Seth asked.

"I was coming into town to find you. You'd better follow me. There's been a break-in at the house. Your house."

Seth didn't waste time with talking. "We're behind you, let's go."

Abel was half drowsy but he perked up at Jacob's words. "What's wrong, *Mamm*?"

Seth caught Grace's hand and then spoke to Abel. "It'll be all right, *sohn*."

"It's likely some teenagers fooling around," Alice muttered.

Seth nodded, hoping what they were saying proved

true in some regard. The look on Jacob's face was ominous, and he knew his brother too well to not understand what was left unsaid. They'd never had a break-in, or trouble of any sort. One face came to Seth's mind: the leering countenance of Tobias Beiler.

Grace turned to Alice and Violet as the buggy approached the farm. "Please," she whispered. "Take Abel down to see the horses or for a little walk while we see what's to be done."

She saw her son off with a quick hug, then followed Jacob and Seth up the steps to the porch. Mary and Samuel Wyse stood in the light of a lantern and looked hard at Seth.

"*Sohn*," Samuel said. "Maybe Grace might wait here with us—"

"*Nee, danki*," Grace replied before Seth could answer. "I would see, *sei so gut.*"

Samuel nodded and held the screen door wide. Grace entered with Seth's hand on her waist. Everything in the living room and kitchen seemed in order.

"It's the master bedroom," Jacob said in a grim voice as he entered close behind them.

Grace swallowed, and they moved as a group to survey the normally pristine master bedroom. There was chaos everywhere. Furniture splintered, glass shattered, and Seth's clothes and personal possessions strewn everywhere. Grace's clothes hung untouched.

"Well," Seth said. "I suppose my stuff needed a good airing. It's nothing that can't be fixed, Grace."

She shook her head, her eyes filling with tears. "You know it was him, Seth. Maybe we should call the police."

"*Nee*," Seth said. "Jacob and I will talk with the bishop. We will handle this."

Grace felt a sick knot forming in the pit of her stomach. But she nodded in agreement and set about helping the others put the room to rights.

Tobias looked down at the page in his journal:

> *She dances and I pull the string*
> *Bald choruses while the wolf waits*
> *Again the feast, for one*
> *And love garners richer hate*

After today, she knew he was close. Close enough to do whatever he wanted, whenever he wanted to do it. All he had to do now was keep up the tension, tighten the circle, and wait for her to come to him.

CHAPTER 36

"What we need around here is some cheerfulness of the spirit," Alice announced one morning, a few days after the break-in. She sat at the kitchen table sniffing Pink Lady cologne samples while Abel lay on the couch next to the dog and Grace puttered at the quilt frame. Violet sat staring at nothing in particular.

"How can we be cheerful?" Abel asked suddenly. "Somebody bad came here."

Alice considered. "True, but we were not at home, and that's a blessing. We're all fine, Abel. God is good."

"*Jah,*" Grace sighed. "Alice is right, Abel. Listen well."

"I'm going out," the child replied.

"You may," Grace said, a gentle reproach. "But play near the house, all right?"

"Why?"

"Because your mama says so," Alice said.

The screen door banged behind the boy, and Pretty followed him to the door. Alice watched Grace go and let the dog out, then turned from her fragrant samples.

"Grace, it may not be my business, but your husband's been looking glummer than a kid who has to celebrate a birthday and Christmas at the same time. All right, Seth isn't saying it, but we know that crazy

Tobias is probably somehow involved. He always made me feel weird when I worked at your old home. And now you're starting to fret and worry—and you and Seth are newlyweds, for heaven's sake! Act like it! Pull your man up a bit, why don't you? It's what I did with Bud when he'd come home late from the railroad. I'd have a nice dinner waiting for him, maybe some kissing—"

She stopped and shook her head. "I'm being foolish, I suppose, but I don't want to see you waste any time that you have together—none of it."

Grace stood up and came over to give her a big hug. "You're right, Alice. God doesn't want us to live in fear."

"Amen to that." Alice smiled. "Now, how about testing some of this honeysuckle piña colada cologne?"

Grace decided that Alice might have a point. She made an especially good lunch for Seth: mayonnaise cake, potato salad, grilled pork chops, and fresh chopped broccoli, with a mason jar of wild roses in water, all waiting for him on the table.

"Well." He smiled. "What's the special occasion? And where are Alice and Violet and Abel?"

"They ate earlier," Grace said. "Alice offered to go on a hunt for baby frogs with Abel. I wanted some time for us to talk."

"Okay," Seth said, washing his hands at the sink. "Are we talking about something serious?"

"Well, I wanted to thank you again for doing all of that paperwork to set up adopting Abel." Grace paused, remembering the day at the courthouse in Lockport. "I thought perhaps it would do us both good to have some time . . ." She paused. "Alone."

Grace saw a genuine smile on his face for the first time in days.

Seth finished his meal and pushed aside his plate. "Let's talk about kissing," he said.

She ducked her head. "I'd rather not."

"I know," he said. "But sooner or later we're going to do it again. And trust me, we're going to *want* to do it again. God designed our bodies and minds to want to kiss, to show affection, tenderness . . . maybe to heal."

She put a hand to her lips, her eyes far away, as if seeing something dark and hopeless.

Seth steeled himself to go on. "Did Silas Beiler kiss you?"

She dropped her hand and met his gaze squarely. "He did not kiss me—not the way you mean. Not with any tenderness or love."

Seth remembered the dream of his wedding night, the sinister shadow coming between him and his bride.

"I used to kiss the rose petals when I was a girl." She made the confession in a rush, and he felt tenderness and a tightening in his chest at her words. It was the first time she'd mentioned her life before Beiler.

He picked a full red rose from the jar on the table, stripped off the tiny thorns, and handed it across to her. "Take it," he said in a whisper. "Remember how it felt. And know that, like this rose without its thorns, I will do my best to bring you joy and never pain."

Grace looked into the earnest, expectant eyes of her husband and took the rose from him. She leaned into its petals and inhaled its fragrance, breathing in the rich aromas of summer and delight and possibility. She felt the velvety petals against her skin and brushed her lips across the petals.

"Thank you," she said.

And she closed her eyes, trying to remember the girl she had been once, a lifetime ago, when she had loved to kiss the flowers.

CHAPTER 37

Jacob stopped by that evening, obviously in a hurry. "Hiya," he said. "Would you do me a favor and check on Lilly in a bit? Her *mamm's* not home, and I'm going to be gone late. I've heard of an abused gelding down in Boalsville, and I want to see if I can get ahold of him."

"Sure thing," Seth promised.

As Jacob left, everyone followed him out onto the porch to wish him well. Seth sniffed the air. "It's going to be a doozy of a storm."

"How do you know?" Alice asked.

Seth gestured with his hand. "You can see it gathering over the mountains. See that gray line in those clouds? You can almost feel it."

"I can smell it," Abel said. "I smell rain in the air. It smells good."

"I love a thunderstorm," Grace said.

"You are full of surprises," Seth said. "I thought most women were afraid of lightning and thunder. It gets really loud here in the valley."

"Good," she said. "The louder, the better." Grace smiled. "When there was a storm in Middle Hollow, I used to go out on the porch and watch it roll in."

"I went with you," Abel said.

"Yes, you did. We would stand and watch the power of the storm, and marvel at what God is like."

"Well, in that case, do you want to come with me to stop in on Lilly?"

"Yes, you two go on. Abel and I will watch from the front porch," Alice said. "I don't know where Violet's gotten off to."

Grace smiled. "She'll come home like a jackrabbit soon enough. She doesn't like storms one bit. Don't worry about her, Alice."

Violet drew rein on the small buggy as the first ominous raindrops began to strike. She had pulled up right outside the Kings' large barns, but no one seemed to be about.

"All right, Amy," she said to Grace's horse. "Looks like it's you and me." She tried to keep her voice level, to keep the nervous horse calm until she could get inside. But before she could slide down from the buggy seat, someone grasped her around the waist.

"It's foolish to drive about when this kind of a storm is coming."

She turned to face Luke, ignoring the flash of lightning that normally would have had her running for cover. The flash in his eyes was much more worth her attention. He caught the reins and began to pull both her and the horse toward the barn.

"We need shelter for the horse," he called over the thunder. "Now!"

She nodded and followed him inside.

Luke had thought endlessly of the kiss he'd shared with Violet behind the feed store; it had kept him awake at night. And now, being alone in the sheltered intimacy of the barn, all he wanted to do was kiss her again. But he felt at odds with himself when he was around her, unable to resolve the conflicting feelings when she looked at him with her sea-blue eyes.

He unhitched the mare and led her into an empty stall. He took his time, not looking at Violet, but vividly aware of her presence. He wished he had someone to talk things over with. His *bruders*, unfortunately, would tease him mercilessly, and he wasn't prepared for that.

Then he lifted his head and gave a speculative glance at the object of his dilemma. Maybe . . . maybe he could talk with her.

As the clouds gathered and the thunder began to rumble from beyond the mountains, Seth and Grace headed to the buggy.

Grace relished the storm as they drove. The wildness and the freedom of it were a bit different here in the mountain. The lightning strikes were more pronounced, the thunder deeper. And she loved it all.

Within a few minutes they arrived at Jacob's house. They knocked on the door, but no one answered.

"That's odd," Seth said. He turned the doorknob and it gave. Inside, the house was dark, with only one kerosene lamp burning on the kitchen sink.

"Lilly?" Seth called.

"In here," a fragile voice responded.

They went into the living room to find Lilly lying on the couch. "Seth, Grace. Thank God."

"Are you all right?" Seth asked.

"Can I talk to Grace for a minute—in private?"

Seth nodded and backed away into the kitchen with a worried look on his face.

Lilly held out a hand and Grace took it. "Grace, something's wrong," Lilly said. "I'm bleeding. A lot."

"Do you need an ambulance?"

She shook her head. "No. Have Seth go for the midwife."

"I'll get him." She ran to the kitchen, where Seth paced anxiously. "Lilly needs the midwife. Now!"

Seth looked at her in alarm and nodded. "I'll go." He was out the door in a second, running through sheets of rain to the buggy.

Grace grabbed the lamp and went back to the couch. "Are you in pain?"

Lilly nodded. "It started about half an hour after Jacob left. I went to the bathroom, and I knew something was wrong." Her voice broke.

"How far along are you?"

"Three months . . . only three months."

"Just hang on, Lilly. We're getting help."

Grace held her hand and stroked her hair and listened to the rain beat down. Finally she heard the sound of hoofbeats above the storm. Seth came in with *Fraa* Knepp, both of them drenched to the skin. The midwife called for more light, then did a brief examination of Lilly while Seth and Grace waited anxiously in the kitchen.

She soon called them back.

"She's definitely miscarrying, but we'll have to wait. These things can take some time. The best we can do is make her comfortable and be here for her." She turned back to Lilly. "I'm going to stay with you and give you something for the pain."

Grace went to sit by Lilly. She did not know what it was like to have a miscarriage, but she could imagine.

"Rachel," Lilly said. "I wanted to name her Rachel. I was sure it was a girl. Rachel Wyse, that would have been so pretty." She looked over Grace's shoulder at Seth. "I wish Jacob were here."

"I can go try to find him," Seth said. "He went to Boalsville, that's all I know."

But before he could say another word, the kitchen door banged open.

Jacob had arrived.

Jacob stood for a minute looking around the room. He was soaking wet and dripping on the floor.

"What's going on?" he asked. "Why is everybody here?"

Seth started toward him, but Jacob caught sight of Lilly and pushed past his brother to kneel beside the couch.

"Jacob, I lost the baby. I thought it was going to be a girl—I'm so sorry."

"Why are you sorry? Don't be—" The words caught in his throat, and he began to cry.

Jacob laid his head down against Lilly's breast, and

Seth looked away. He caught Grace's eye and nodded toward the kitchen.

They went out onto the porch. Thunder shook the hills and lightning flashed, and the rain continued to fall. Grace touched his arm. He looked down at her and didn't even try to hide the tears. "I wanted to be an uncle," he said.

"I know," she said. "And I know how much you hurt for Jacob and Lilly. I know how much Jacob means to you."

She put her arms around him and he hugged her tightly, letting his tears fall on her shoulder. He wanted to stay there forever, in the warmth of her arms, while the storm raged around them.

But the moment passed. The door opened behind them, and Grace stepped back. Jacob appeared, his face ashen and strained. "Please, both of you, come back inside for a while. We want you."

By the time *Fraa* Knepp's duties were completed, Lilly had fallen into an exhausted sleep and Jacob sat holding her hand. Seth came and put his arm around his brother.

"She was so happy about this baby." Jacob stared into the burning lamp. "There will be other pregnancies, right?" he asked *Fraa* Knepp.

The midwife nodded. "There's absolutely no reason she can't have another child."

He rose suddenly. "I'm going to go put up the horse."

Seth followed him, walking slowly through the lessening storm. He helped with the chores in the warm comfort of the barn, and when everything was done, he turned and extended his arms to his brother. Jacob came into the hug without resistance and rested his head on Seth's shoulder. It was a rare moment between them. Seth felt some part of himself grow up, as if for the first time he understood that loss could mean growth.

"I wanted this baby," Jacob said.

"I know," Seth whispered. "Me too."

Jacob breathed a huge sigh, then stepped back from his brother. He gave Seth a weak smile. "But we'll try again, as the Lord wills, and have some joy in the trying."

When Seth finally felt comfortable enough to leave, he got the buggy out of the barn, took the midwife home, and rode back to the farm in silence with Grace close at his side.

The days ahead would be hard for Lilly and Jacob. But he and Grace would visit often and do what they could to ease the pain of loss.

It was what families did for one another.

Violet watched as Luke moved from her to sit on a hay bale, leaning his back against a barn beam.

"So," he began in a conversational tone, "the truth of the matter is that I understand farming. Not women."

Violet went to stand opposite him. "Women aren't so much difficult, not if you're careful."

He shook his head. "I'm at a loss," he whispered against the roll of the thunder. "That kiss the other day. The buggy ride. You—someone as beautiful as you—wanting me."

"It was the caterpillar."

He arched a dark brow. "You're telling me that all of this, this goings-on, is because of a baby caterpillar?"

Violet nodded and came forward to sit beside him on the hay bale. "You see, women want to be seen, noticed, and nurtured—like you did with the baby caterpillar."

"I'm confused."

She reached a hand up to touch his face. "Don't be. Maybe . . . maybe I shouldn't have started this."

He shook his head and turned his face so that his lips touched her palm. *"Nee,"* he muttered. "Maybe not."

They returned home late, but Grace couldn't unwind to go to sleep. Instead she stood on the porch watching the storm dissipate. The trees ceased to bend and the rustling corn stilled.

Seth came and stood beside her. "The storm is passing," she said.

"I know," Seth replied.

"And it will pass for Lilly and Jacob."

"I know."

It was the Amish way to accept loss as part of life, to trust that *Gott* knew best. But it wasn't easy.

Seth put his arm around Grace and she leaned into him. Together they stood watching as the last of the clouds drifted away into the night and the stars came out once again.

CHAPTER 38

Grace dressed for Sunday Meeting and battled within herself. On the one hand, she didn't especially want to see Kate Zook at Meeting that morning. The girl was cynical and wounded. Grace understood this, but the understanding was no help. She couldn't get past the way Kate looked at Seth.

On the other hand, maybe she should befriend the girl instead of being jealous of her.

Grace resolved to talk to Kate before church Meeting. Neither Seth's past nor her own should control the way she lived in the present.

Later, as they were sitting down to breakfast, Alice came into the kitchen wearing a wild pink hat and carrying her Pink Lady sales bag. "Well," Alice said, "I wonder if someone might accompany me to church in town?" The flowers on her hat bobbed in time to her words. "I noticed it the other day. White, and sits on a corner?"

Grace was a bit disappointed. She could have used Alice's support, because she never knew how long Abel would sit still for the Meeting. Sometimes he could make it through the whole two hours, but there were other times when she had to take him out so that he could walk around or do something quietly. The community never called any attention to their comings and goings, but it still sometimes bothered Grace. And Violet could be no help, as she was meant to sit in a separate section with the other unmarried girls.

Seth came close to her and spoke in a low voice while she washed dishes at the sink. "What do you think about me going with Alice?"

Grace said, "Well, it's a church, and life is about a relationship with God, not any certain religion. You go on. We'll be fine."

"Okay," Seth said. He offered an arm to Grace and then to Alice, who took it with a charmed smile.

After Seth dropped them off, Grace steered Abel into the Zooks' home, hosts of the church Meeting that week. She was glad she did not encounter Kate Zook right off. At prayer during the week, she had felt a definite nudging, a sense of calling to pursue a relationship with the girl. To try to help her somehow.

At first there was the normal hubbub and chattering. Grace told Abel to find a quiet place on the end of the bench so they could slip out if necessary. He took her bag and sat down. She saw him begin to root through the bag, already looking for pretzels or something to snack on. His anxious eyes scanned the crowd. Large groups were difficult for Abel, no matter how supportive the people were.

Grace began to walk among the benches, nodding

briefly to women here and there. Then finally she saw
Kate—coming right toward her. The girl's green eyes
seemed alight with a flame. She certainly was beautiful, Grace thought again, but there was a malicious
intent to those pretty eyes.

"Where is your husband?" Kate asked.

Grace inhaled a deep, steadying breath and prayed
that God would give her the words to say. She motioned
the girl over into a corner. "Kate, I want to tell you
something."

"Having marriage problems and need some advice?"
Kate asked.

Grace smiled and shook her head. "No. I want to tell
you about my husband sometime."

"Oh, I already know all about Seth," Kate said.

"No. I mean my first husband." With that one sen-
tence, Grace had Kate's undivided attention. Half the
people in the community wanted to know what had
happened with her first husband. "I have never revealed
any major details," she said.

"Why would you want to tell me?"

"Because," Grace said, "you know how things get
around. I'd like to lay to rest some of the rumors I've
heard about myself. And my sister, Violet, is about your
age. She could use a friend. I thought you might come
over and help me quilt one day next week. I'm working
on a new quilt for Seth."

"Oh, well, if it's for Seth—surely."

Grace did not miss the girl's sarcastic attitude, but
she didn't mind. She felt driven to offer this strange girl
a peace that she did not necessarily feel herself.

Kate walked away and Grace joined Abel on the bench.

She wondered how Seth was faring.

Seth drove his buggy up behind a long line of cars at the small white church. He had never been inside but had often thought it pretty, with its white clapboard and colorful borders of flowers.

"Come on." Alice nudged him. "Let's go in."

Seth was not used to feeling self-conscious, but he felt it now—an *Amisch* man usually did not go to another service. But Grace was right. It was a church just the same. So he followed as Alice walked up the stone steps to the double doors.

Inside, the church smelled of fresh beeswax. Alice went around distributing her Pink Lady brochures to some friends she'd made in town. He saw Viv, not realizing that this was where she worshipped.

"What are you doing here?" she asked.

"Passing through."

He crossed his arms in front of his chest, trying to hide his suspenders, as the other men wore suits and ties.

Viv patted his arm. "Well, I'm glad to have you. Pastor O'Reilly always gives a great sermon."

"*Gut,*" Seth answered.

Alice led them up the aisle to the middle pews. He sat down and stared forward. There was a large cross on the wall. A choir was singing softly in the background—a small choir with pleasant voices, accompanied by an organ. Seth enjoyed the music, even though his people had no musical instruments in their worship.

Alice leaned over and whispered in his ear, "Try to relax and get some meaning out of this for your life. You never know what you might learn in a strange environment."

There were hymns and some prayers, and then the choir sang again. Finally Pastor O'Reilly, a rotund man with a balding head, went to the pulpit, opened a small Bible, and began to read:

For I am convinced that neither death nor life, neither angels nor demons, neither the present nor the future, nor any powers, neither height nor depth, nor anything else in all creation, will be able to separate us from the love of God that is in Christ Jesus our Lord.

Seth knew the verses, but he had never heard anyone talk about them in the way that Pastor O'Reilly began to do.

"The key word in these verses is *love*," Pastor O'Reilly said. He smiled out at the congregation. "The love of God. The love of God is eternal, and it is fierce in power. It gives us hope when loved ones die, that although they are not present in body, we are still connected to them through this love."

Alice felt her throat tighten up. She didn't want to hear the pastor's words, but they went right to her soul. Did

God have to bring her hundreds of miles from home to tell her something? Maybe she hadn't been willing to listen to Him in the past. Or maybe the distractions of life and death and grief just got in the way.

She ducked her head and dabbed at her eyes with a lavender hankie. If she really believed that she and Bud were still connected somehow, she might not be as afraid on her own, or as lonely. She looked back up at the pastor and then at the cross. What was it the Bible said about Jesus? *"He was a man of sorrows and acquainted with grief."* She hadn't thought of that verse in years. Maybe that was the trick, to make grief's acquaintance, become friends with it even.

Suddenly the prospect of being alone didn't seem so awful. It seemed, well, like a chance to grow.

As Seth listened to the man's words, he couldn't help but think about the apparent separation between him and Grace. Was God promising that nothing could separate them through Christ?

Seth took a leap of faith and began to pray silently for his marriage. He prayed that God would give him the wisdom and the maturity to be the kind of husband Grace needed. He prayed for Grace, that God would heal her and give her peace. He prayed for Lilly and Jacob. If what Pastor O'Reilly said was true, then nothing could separate Lilly from the baby she had lost.

It was a thought to share with people back home.

The service went on with various phrases and responses. Seth understood this. He knew what it was to respond to an affirmation or exhortation from the bishop or deacons. But during the songs, he just listened, taking in the words and the music and the beauty of it all.

Afterward, as they milled outside, Alice looked up at him. "What did you think of your first *Englisch* service?"

"I thought it was good, but I thought the communion was weird," he said. "What were those little white circles?"

She laughed and patted him on the arm. "I'll tell you in the buggy."

CHAPTER 39

Tobias Beiler waited until the procession of buggies had lined up and everyone was inside the great barn, then he loped off through the cornfield to the Wyse home. He'd saved a chicken bone from his supper the night before. Once the dog was pacified, it was nothing to pick the lock on the back door again.

He made his way to the master bedroom and eased open the door, feeling a rush of desire at being so near where she slept each night. In the first bureau drawer he found men's clothes, neatly folded. Impatiently he pushed them aside and moved down to the next drawer.

There he found Grace's handkerchiefs. He caught up a handful and pulled them to his face.

"Soon, my sweet," he whispered.

Bishop Loftus had a fire in his eye about something. It was very rare that the little man lectured the community or took them to task. But as he began to speak in a stern voice, it was apparent that there was an issue to be addressed.

"I'd like to talk to you today," he began, "about

something common to all of us, and yet uncommon to some of us. I'd like to talk to you about water."

There was a general mumbling of interest as the bishop continued.

"The Lord baptized with water. Jesus called Himself the living water. But it has come to my attention that there is another body of water in our community in which the people have been indulging, and I'm afraid I must take offense."

Suddenly Grace knew what he was going to say. She glanced, as did everyone, at Emily Mast and her young husband, Peter. They had bought an *Englisch* home that had an in-ground swimming pool. All the teenagers loved to go there and were wearing bathing suits. The bishop must've gotten wind of it.

Bishop Loftus continued, "I don't mind wading in the creek, so long as you're in some clothes, and I don't mind swimming in the bathtub on a Saturday night." By now the people were quietly murmuring, shuffling. "But I'm afraid I do mind a swimming pool. It's a temptation for our youth, so if any of you have a swimming pool at your disposal, might I suggest that in the next week you plow over it and turn it into a late field of corn and stop this nonsense. Thank you."

And that, Grace knew, would be the end of the in-ground swimming pool.

"I'm glad I went with you this morning," Seth said to Alice. "But I'm also glad we'll be back in time for gathering."

"What's gathering?" Alice said.

"After Sunday Meeting we relax and eat some good food and play volleyball," he explained.

"Volleyball? You think these legs can play volleyball?" She showed him a rather sleek ankle in nylons.

"Well, maybe." Seth grinned and the two laughed together.

"I like you, Pretty Boy," Alice said.

"Thank you, ma'am. I like you too." He helped Alice down from the buggy, scanning the crowd. Abel sat off by himself in the crook of an apple tree. He knew the boy didn't especially love crowds, so the tree was probably giving him solace. When he found Grace, she was sitting with Kate Zook. He approached the table, and Kate got up to go. For once, she passed him without comment.

He put one leg over the bench seat and sat down. "Hiya, what was that about?"

"Oh, woman talk. You wouldn't be interested." Grace smiled.

"I'm interested in anything that has to do with you."

"That's the way to greet a woman," Alice announced behind them. "Now, where do I get the food?"

"Right over there." Seth pointed to a table lined up with various good-looking casseroles and hardy bowls.

Alice went off, her Pink Lady bag still over her arm.

"I'm glad you invited her," Seth said. "I think she'll find it easy to be accepted among these women. They know she's newly widowed, and they'll be kind to her."

"You do realize that she's going to give Pink Lady books to everyone?" Grace asked.

Seth smiled at her. "Then maybe we'll have some better-looking and-smelling *Amisch* people."

Grace laughed. "You're impossible."

Seth watched Grace's eyes following Abel over at the apple tree. "Abel goes off by himself so much. It's the crowd, you know. And he likes to climb the tree to feel the pressure of the limbs against him. I read about it once. It's called deep pressure, and it's something that autistic people often find calming."

"Well, if it comforts him, then that's good."

He felt her eyes on him. "Seth, you are so good about understanding Abel. You're an excellent father."

He leaned across the table and drew her fingers to his lips. "And you are the best mother I know." Then he let her go and grinned. "I'm going to go get some food. Do you want anything else?"

He joined the line at the table in time to hear Alice trying to sell *Fraa* Esh some beauty cream.

"It'll take ten years off your face," Alice whispered loudly. Seth saw *Fraa* Esh glance around furtively, then take a book of Pink Lady products. Alice moved on to her next victim.

Seth filled his plate with fried chicken, potato salad, macaroni salad, broccoli salad, and green salad, then grabbed a cup of sweet tea and made his way back to Grace.

He had barely sat down when she rose with her plate. "I'm sorry, Seth," she said, "but it's my turn to help with the dishes. Can you check on Abel after you've eaten?"

He nodded with a smile, then watched her walk away to where tubs of soapy water were lined up. The thought ran through his mind that there was no one more beautiful than she was, both inside and outside.

He walked over to the tree to see what Abel was doing. Abel was compressed between two branches, his legs dangling, his chest pressed tightly against the wood.

"That feel good, *sohn*?" he asked.

"*Jah*, it makes me feel calm in my belly."

Seth thought for a minute. "You don't like to be around the crowd especially, do you?"

"*Nee*," Abel said. "Too many people. Too many eyes."

"What do you mean?"

"I feel like all their eyes look at me. They look at me and I can't look them in the eyes."

"You can if you choose, maybe," Seth said. "You're brave, remember?"

"Yeah, but this isn't about being brave. This is about I don't want to look them in the eye."

Grace reached into a bucket of soapy water and began to wash the dishes and silverware. Suddenly big boots and a pair of blue jeans appeared in her line of vision. She shielded her eyes with a dripping hand. "Hello?"

A large, tanned hand was thrust at her. "Hi, I'm Nick. I work with the local volunteer fire company. We're here to talk about getting the mud sale and dinner together in a couple of weeks. I, uh, wondered if you'd be there?"

She shook hands, hers still damp, then went back to washing dishes. "I'll be there."

"Great." The dark-haired man grinned.

She arched a brow at him. "But so will my husband."

"Oh, uh, you're married. You, uh, look so young, I thought . . ."

"What did you think?"

Grace straightened at the dangerously soft sound of her husband's voice behind her. She glanced over her shoulder and saw that Seth was staring intently at the other man, his blue eyes ice cold.

"Uh, nothing, man. I mean . . . I'm sorry. Husband, right?" Nick's hand shot out again. "No hard feelings?"

Seth laughed then, apparently abandoning the jealous husband role. The two men began to talk and joke together. Soon Seth was leading the fireman to the food table.

Alice sidled up beside her, eating a piece of raisin pie. "Luring him away toward other prey."

"What?" Grace asked.

Alice took a big bite. "Seth's leading him to other food to feast his eyes upon."

"*Ach*," Grace murmured. She would never understand the ways of men.

A few minutes later Seth lightly touched her waist. "So you're chatting up the local firemen now?"

She reared up and looked him in the eye. "No."

"I'm just kidding, Grace. I know you weren't doing anything wrong."

"Silas would have—"

He put two fingers against her lips. "I can imagine what he would've done, but remember—I'm not him. I'm never going to be him."

"I know," Grace said.

He took her hand, and they walked over to where Abel sat in the apple tree.

"Abel, we're going to go over and visit *Onkel* Jacob and *Aenti* Lilly," Grace told him.

"How come?" Abel asked.

Grace glanced cautiously at Seth. "Well," she said, "Lilly was going to have a baby but she lost it."

Abel peered at her curiously. "Where'd she lose it?"

"No," Grace said, trying again. "You see, the Lord decided she wasn't going to have it anymore."

"Why would He do that?" the boy said. "That's not very nice."

"The Lord is always good, Abel," Seth said. "Even when we can't understand Him. It's like—it's like your mama's quilting. At first you can't tell the pattern she's sewing, right?"

Abel rocked against the tree. "Yeah, it looks like a mess."

"Well, that's how it is with the Lord. He can take something that looks like a mess to us and turn it into something beautiful. You know?"

Abel shrugged. "I didn't know *Gott* makes quilts. I'm going to make *Aenti* Lilly a card."

"That would be great." Grace was proud of her son for thinking of such an idea. Then she turned to Seth. "Thank you," she whispered.

"For what?"

"For cherishing our wedding promise so dearly."

She watched him flush with color, and he nodded vaguely.

"Hey," Abel cried. "Can I paint it? Can I paint the card?"

Grace looked at Seth and noticed his jaw tighten.

"Maybe not, my sweet. You can be so much more personal—more you—with a drawing."

"That's not always true," Seth said evenly.

Grace could tell that he was not going to let the matter drop.

Alice came up and joined them. "Well, I got ten new Pink Lady customers. The collagen-boosting products are going to do well among the Amish."

Grace forced a smile and tried to concentrate on her friend's words—anything to avoid the storm she felt was coming with Seth.

When they arrived home, Abel scurried off in search of paper and pencils. Alice went up to her room to plot her new Pink Lady orders, and Violet, as usual, was off somewhere. Grace hadn't seen her since the Meeting.

Grace sank down onto the couch. She was always tired after sitting on the backless benches of Meeting. And although the gatherings were fun, they too seemed tiring today.

Seth sat down in the chair opposite her. "Grace, you know he could've painted the card."

"He could have," she murmured.

"What's the difference between painting and doing a coloring book?"

"I don't want to talk about this."

"Well, we need to talk about it," Seth said. "You have to understand that this is part of who I am."

Grace opened her eyes. "But it's a secret part."

"Oh, and you don't have secrets?"

"Yes, I have secrets, but I don't want to keep them."

"That's not true." He shook his head. "You want to keep them like the bear that's got hold of the beehive. He may get stung to death, but sometimes it's a reflex not to let go."

"That's not fair, Seth. It's not fair to compare what happened to me for nine years to your painting."

"Why not?"

"I don't know. Because what you do makes you happy. It wasn't the same for me."

He moved suddenly, kneeling in front of her and framing her with his long arms. He looked up earnestly into her face. "I'd like to make you happy, Grace," he said.

She gazed down at him in confusion; this was more difficult than the idea of him losing his temper. "Seth, I don't know what—"

"I just want to love you and understand you better," he went on. "This painting thing is important because it's a source of tension between us."

"Seth, I can't agree with you because I don't know what the bishop would—"

She broke off as Abel came running into the room with his hand-drawn card. He went to Seth. "I made a tree for *Aenti* Lilly, and I put a baby under the tree so a new baby will grow—maybe as big as the tree."

"It's fine, *sohn*. She'll love it."

Grace noticed, with some hurt, that Abel did not tilt the card toward her.

CHAPTER 40

Seth went to the bedroom to change his shirt. He picked a green one to wear to Jacob's, then happened to glance at the bureau drawers. One of them was half-open and askew instead of neatly closed as both he and Grace kept them.

He felt a chill go down his spine. Tobias Beiler had surely been in the house again. He closed his eyes, trying to think, trying to pray. Then he heard Grace knock softly on the door.

"Seth, I—are you angry? Please, may I come in?"

He hurried to close the drawers, then went to open the door. She looked up at him with anxious eyes.

"I'm coming, Grace. I'm almost ready. Please, go outside with Abel and get in the buggy. I'll be along."

Seth drove without thinking, his mind occupied with other things. How could he make his home more secure without alarming Grace and Abel? How could he reconcile this disagreement with Grace about the painting?

All husbands and wives had disagreements, but the painting seemed so fundamental, so intrinsically part of who he was. There was a time when Lilly had actually wanted him to come to the school and teach the children how to do it. But his own wife . . . it felt as if she wanted to take something from him. Something precious.

Yet his conscience prodded him. He wanted to take her past from her. And how much more problematic and wrenching a thing to take from someone . . .

He glanced sideways at her and reached out to grasp her hand. She turned to look at him.

"I'm sorry," he said softly.

She nodded. "Me too."

It made him feel a bit better, but it did nothing to resolve the deeper issue.

When they arrived at Lilly and Jacob's, Grace was surprised to be greeted with smiles from both of them. Lilly looked wan and pale but still happy somehow. Jacob, too, had a peacefulness about him as Grace presented the various casseroles that had been given that afternoon as tokens of love and goodwill.

"Sit down, *sei so gut*," Jacob invited. "We have a lot to tell you."

"How are you, Lilly?" Grace asked softly.

"I am well. We both prayed about this last night and feel that this is not so much a loss but an opportunity for us to grow closer in love."

Grace saw Seth pass a hand over his eyes. "A painful opportunity, though. We are so sorry," he said.

Jacob laid a hand on his brother's shoulder. "Don't,

Seth. It's all right, really. There will be plenty of other chances for you to be an *onkel*."

Grace smiled at her brother-in-law. "You are both so brave."

Lilly shook her head. "*Nee*. We know there will still be much grieving to come, but when the Lord takes away, He always gives back. We need to believe that."

"Well, you're stronger in your faith than I am." Seth caught his *bruder* close for a hug and then came to Lilly to do the same. Grace embraced them both, then gave Seth a look to say they probably should leave.

Jacob led them to the door and caught Grace's arm. "Visit, Grace, will you? She'll need it later."

"I give my word," Grace said. She followed Seth to the buggy.

They didn't talk much on the ride home. Seth seemed deep in thought—probably marveling, as she was, at the united front Jacob and Lilly brought to their difficult situation.

Seth pulled the buggy close to the house and came around to help Grace down. When he touched her arm, she felt the warmth of his hand linger, almost as if he were touching her to make sure she was real.

She wanted to comfort him somehow, say something, but then her feet touched the ground and the moment had passed.

Seth unhitched the horse and saw to its needs without a thought to what he was doing. He felt tired and drained. The loss of Jacob and Lilly's baby had affected him more than he realized, and he wondered, for the first time in his life, about the sovereign hand of *Gott*.

He'd heard other people pose such questions: *If God is good, then why does He let bad things happen?* Seth didn't know the answers, not by a long shot. But he had seen how the foal sometimes did not get to its feet, could not nurse, was turned on by its mother . . .

This was all part of nature, and the mystery of things unseen.

But still it didn't answer the unanswerable question. He thought about the quilt image he'd given Abel earlier—the pattern that only God could see.

Perhaps it was the best he could do.

Grace looked up as her father-in-law came in the door.

"Hiya," Samuel Wyse said. "Mary's having a nap. She spent a couple of hours with Lilly early this morning, and I thought I'd look for some coffee and a bit of company."

"Sit down." Grace waved him to the table. "Please."

"How about some baked beans too?" Alice offered. "I made them this afternoon. Baked beans are a great comfort food, and you folks could sure use a bit of comforting." She slid a plate in front of Samuel as Grace filled his cup.

Seth came in, greeted his *daed*, then went to the sink to wash up. Grace went to his side and touched his arm lightly.

"Seth, do you want some coffee?"

"*Jah, danki.*"

For once he wasn't looking intensely at her, but seemed distant and removed. He sat down across from his father and Alice plied him with baked beans.

"What ails you, *sohn*?" Samuel asked.

Seth let out a breath. "I'm struggling, I guess, trying to figure out why Lilly lost the baby. I'm weary of hearing that sometimes what looks like a mess is really God's will."

His *daed* nodded. "In the middle of the mess, Seth, there is majesty."

"I don't know."

"There're some so-called Christians who would say she lost the baby because of sin in her life—that God is punishing her for something unconfessed," Alice said.

"Silas Beiler would have said that too," Grace added softly. "He believed that misfortune befell people because they deserved it for sinning."

"I don't understand how someone could be that off in the head, in the heart, to consider such a thing." Seth's voice was tight. "Jacob and Lilly are *gut* people, the finest I know."

"*Sohn*." Samuel laid a weathered hand on Seth's arm. "This is not about punishment."

"What's it about, then?"

"Sometimes bad things happen in our lives," Samuel went on. "What matters most is how we respond to the bad things. Now, I could say that I've been cheated out of a grandbaby and spend my time being mad at God, or I can trust Him that there's something better."

Grace watched Seth draw a deep breath, then he looked straight at her. "The pastor at the church in town talked about how we can't be separated from God's love—nothing can separate us. So I guess this wrestling with *Gott* won't separate me either."

"*Nee,*" Grace whispered. She felt a surge of hope when she saw the spark return to his blue eyes.

Nothing can separate us . . .

CHAPTER 41

The next day a pink flyer arrived, advertising the annual mud sale and spaghetti dinner that the *Amisch* would host in conjunction with the Lockport volunteer fire department.

"It's in two weeks," Alice said. "So tell me about my first mud sale."

Grace refilled their coffee cups.

"I didn't get to go to them in Middle Hollow, but I've heard they are a great place to get just about anything a person could imagine: quilts, preserves, sheds, livestock, cabinets, mirrors, firewood, plants—*ach*, anything!"

"Isn't it a little late for a mud sale?" Alice asked. "The grass is pretty green."

"*Jah*, but this spring was so rainy that the actual mud was too much, so they postponed it. But I expect the ground will get pretty muddy still, with five hundred *Englisch* and *Amisch* people traipsing about."

"I've heard the food is good," Alice said. "What all do they have besides spaghetti?"

"I don't know." Grace smiled. "Pot pie, barbecued chicken, kettle cooked chips—I suppose we will eat ourselves silly."

Alice sighed with satisfaction. "Now that I can do."

When Jacob walked into the barn his first morning back, Seth had to restrain himself from hugging him. He wanted to act normal, to respond like old times. But there was something changed in his brother's face—a calm maturity, as if he'd been tried by fire and not found lacking.

"Hey," Jacob said softly.

"Hey."

Seth cast about for something to say, feeling unusually tentative. Jacob smiled at him.

"Seth, it's all right. You don't have to treat me with kid gloves. I took some time, wrestled it out with Lilly and *der Herr,* and I'm okay."

"I hate to see you hurt. I've always hated it. Like the time you had your ribs broken by that stallion—"

"But this didn't break me, I promise. Now, tell me how Grace is and how things are moving along."

"We fight about the painting. It subsides, then flares up."

"Like many wounds," Jacob observed.

Seth looked at him intently. "My painting is not a wound."

"It's a secret well kept, though. What does the Bible say? 'What I tell you in darkness; proclaim in the light'? Maybe you hug it to yourself, and that contributes to the wound between you and Grace."

In his brother's words, Seth heard an echo of his own accusations to Grace the other night. Had he been doing the very thing he had accused her of?

"You know, your cheek pulses when you think," Jacob said. "I'm surprised *Mamm* and *Daed* never figured it out while you manufactured excuses for our lateness with the girls."

"Yeah, the girls . . ."

"Regrets?"

Seth sighed. "Some."

"Then try to put all of your 'practice' into good experiences for your *fraa*."

"You're right," Seth said. "I guess something positive can come out of this, after all." He grinned at his brother. It was good to feel as if balance had been restored between them.

The day of the sale loomed quickly. With her ankle finally healed and free of the cast, Grace had spent much of the week making baked goods to be auctioned off.

"All of the money goes to support the volunteer fire department," Grace told Alice. "We're really blessed to have them."

"I should say so," Alice said. "You don't need a barn burning around here."

"Whose barn is burning?" Seth asked from the doorway.

He came in and casually brushed his knuckles against Grace's cheek. "There's some stuff up in the attic that *Mamm* and *Daed* want to donate to the sale. Want to come help me look?"

"I don't know," Grace said. "Abel—"

Alice picked up their coffee cups. "You go on. I'll wash these up and then get Abel. I promised to make salty-oily play dough with him this morning."

Grace followed Seth up to the third floor. She hadn't been up in the attic yet, though she knew she would spend a lot of time there in the fall when it was time to dry the root vegetables.

"Jacob and I used to play up here a lot. *Mamm* would have a fit because she was afraid we'd knock the onions down. But mostly we spent time scaring ourselves and fooling around among all of the old chests and things."

Grace was out of breath by the time she gained the top step to the attic.

"It's a climb, isn't it?"

Grace nodded. She stood there for a minute, gazing around at the wide expanse of the center room. Remnants of dried vegetables still lined the edges of the walls. There were several old trunks and a massive wardrobe against one wall.

"There are two other side rooms off of this one." Seth opened a panel hidden cleverly in the wall, concealing the entrance. He gestured to the opening. "Want to hear a secret?"

"Okay . . ."

Grace lifted her skirt and navigated through the space. She could spend days up here, just opening the trunks to see what was inside. But not today.

She stooped to get through the small door in the wall, then stood fully erect and followed her husband.

Sunlight streamed in through a window and played across the dusty wooden floor. Boxes of strange bird feathers were strewn about—even a peacock feather.

"*Daed* used to tie flies," Seth said. "He used the feathers for the lures."

They passed a massive wooden desk, complete with dozens of compartments and cubbyholes. Grace thought it had to have been put together on the spot—she saw no way it would have made it through the door. An old spinning wheel, more chests, and a faded upholstered rocker took up more space.

"This is a huge room."

"I know." Seth smiled at her and dropped into the rocker. He gave it a few experimental moves, apparently pleased with its creaking, then patted his lap.

"Come and sit down," he said. "I want you to hear the secret."

She hesitated, then gingerly smoothed her skirt and perched herself on his knees. "Well, all right . . ."

He pulled her back against his chest and slipped an arm around her.

"Listen," he whispered.

She tried but only heard her heart in her ears. "I'm listening."

"No, really listen."

She closed her eyes and took a breath, and then she heard it: the sound of the faint wind outside whistling like a melody under the narrowed eaves of the room. It was delightful, and if she tried, she could imagine herself atop a mountain with the wind dancing about her, free and beautiful.

"Jacob and I used to come up here at night and scare ourselves with the wind whipping around. Sometimes it sounds like crying, but mostly it's a joy to hear."

She sat listening for a few minutes, gradually pulled

into the warmth of his nearness, the earthy scents of horse and barn and the faint spice of soap.

"What are you thinking about?" he said.

Grace felt like a little girl caught with her hand in a jar of sweets. "Um . . . the sound of the wind."

He laughed low. "Grace Wyse, I do believe that you are sinning." He touched her lips lightly with one finger. "Repeat after me: Thou shalt not lie."

Seth braced his feet on the attic floorboards and tried to focus on the old spring poking him in the back—anything to distract him from the tiny curl that had escaped her *kapp*.

"What are *you* thinking about?" she asked.

"Alas, given your propensity for sin, my sweet, I am forced to tell the truth. I'm thinking about you."

"Well, stop it."

"I can't. Not ever." He rocked forward and nudged her with his chin. "Kiss me," he said.

"From what I hear, you've had more than enough kissing in your short life."

"A fact you should appreciate."

She turned to him with genuine curiosity. "Why?"

"Because I'm *gut* at it."

She gave him an arch look. "I think that's something that a wife should discover for herself."

Seth felt an odd thrill go through his chest and he caught his breath. "So you should." He relaxed back against the rocker and waited.

She laid a hand on his chest and turned toward him, then slowly lowered her lips to his.

He kissed her with all the finesse he could muster, relishing her closeness, her gentleness. Then suddenly she was up and gone from his arms, and his eyes snapped open in dismay.

"What's wrong?"

She looked down at him with a smile. "I think you've had enough practice. I've got to check on the stew."

CHAPTER 42

The day of the mud sale arrived.

"Look at all the buggies and cars," Grace said as they pulled onto Farmer Esh's drive. Hundreds of them, *Amisch* buggies and *Englisch* cars, all gathered together. So many different types of *Amisch* vehicles—some with plush carpeting, brass lanterns, and battery testers; some so shiny they looked brand new. It took them a long time to get parked because Seth and Abel kept stopping to inspect the interiors.

When they actually got to the field, it was already muddy with the pounding of many feet. *Amisch* came from all around to support the volunteer fire department. Many of the *Amisch* volunteered their time alongside the *Englisch*—it was one place where the two communities worked together.

Delicious smells mingled in the air, and Alice took Abel's hand. "What do you say we go get a funnel cake and a snow cone?"

"But it's hardly ten o'clock in the morning," Grace said.

Seth laughed. "It's all right. Go on with Alice, Abel. We'll walk around a little and meet you later."

Grace took Seth's hand. They walked among the crowds, stopping at various vendor booths to look at things. Grace was careful not to pay too much attention to any one item, knowing that Seth would buy it for her if she did. Instead she took pleasure in his company.

But when they came across a booth selling old-fashioned, mother-of-pearl hairbrushes, he wanted to stop. "Whoa, there," he said. "I think we might find something here for you."

"Seth," she whispered, "you know that my hair—"

"Is growing into beguiling ringlets. You need a brush." He pulled her closer to the table and bargained happily for a brush and comb set that the woman wrapped with extra care.

They stepped away from the booth and he bowed to her, presenting her with the package. "My wife."

"*Danki.*"

It was only a brush and comb, but an irrational happiness welled up in her.

She turned to find Abel standing at a display of plastic action figure toys. He looked up, abashed, as they approached.

"Abel," Grace said softly, "come away. Those are graven images."

"They're toys, Grace," Seth said easily, then quickly added, "Obey your mother, *sohn.*"

Abel stepped away but didn't leave. "They scare me."

Seth dropped down on his haunches next to Abel. "They scare you, *sohn*? Why?"

"I don't like their eyes staring at me."

"Your *mamm's* right," Seth said, "those toys are not the best for you. Come on, let's move away."

Abel soon darted ahead, and Grace turned to Seth. "He doesn't like to look people in the eye. Have you noticed that?"

"I know. It's almost like it's too much sensation for him. But he'll gaze into the horses' eyes—and Pretty's."

"Ah, but they're no threat," Grace said.

"It's part of who he is, though. Maybe we can teach him to be more comfortable with it."

"Thank you," Grace said.

"For what?"

She squeezed his hand. "For loving my *sohn*."

Luke King told himself that he needed to get his head on straight where Violet Beiler was concerned.

His family spread out around the grounds of the mud sale, and usually he'd have gone to have a *gut* look at the horses. Instead he found himself combing the crowd for the familiar ivory-skinned face and bright blue eyes.

He found her at a hair ribbon display, pretending nonchalance among the forbidden wares.

"Thinking of a red ribbon?" he whispered in her ear. "Blue would do better."

She spun and slapped playfully at him, and he laughed out loud. It felt good.

"Somebody important you want me to meet?"

Luke paused in his laughter to turn a wary eye on his *bruder* James.

"*Jah*, sure. I'm sure you've seen Violet Beiler at Meeting. She's actually a very distant cousin of ours."

"Dear cousin, let me say hello properly." James made an elaborate show of embracing Violet.

Violet didn't seem to mind James overmuch, but Luke knew he'd take a good ribbing from his brother after the sale. Still, as he gazed at Violet's beautiful face, he decided that it just might be worth it.

He caught her hand firmly in his and raised an eyebrow at James. "If you'll excuse us, we're going to walk about. Together."

Then, turning his back on the look of astonishment that came over James's face, he tucked Violet's hand more firmly into the bend of his arm and strolled away.

The morning passed quickly. Grace and Seth made their way to the auction stand where beautiful quilts were being sold for hundreds of dollars.

"There's not one up there that can compare with your work," Seth whispered softly in his wife's ear.

"What about *your* quilting work?" she teased.

"*Ach*, I prefer when we quilt together. Remind me that we should do that again sometime." He infused his voice with a certain warmth, and she turned to look up at him curiously.

"Why do I think that you're talking about something other than quilting?"

"What else could I possibly mean?" He leaned down and took a quick nip at her neck.

"Seth!" she hissed. "We're in public."

"Sometimes that's half the fun." He offered her his arm. "Come on, let's catch up with the spaghetti dinner. It's not one of my favorites, but it'll do."

"Wait a minute, please. I think I see Kate Zook."

"Kate Zook? Why do you want to talk to her? She's a little pit viper."

"I think I like her." Grace stood on her tiptoes to see better over the crowd. "Let me go speak to her for a minute, please? I'll be right back."

Seth nodded. "All right. I'll wait here by the hunting knives."

He watched Grace make her way through the people and decided once more that he would never, ever understand the ways of women.

"Kate, how are you?"

Grace steeled herself for the girl's negative response. In the preparations for the mud sale, she hadn't found time to follow through on her invitation for Kate to come and quilt.

Kate eyed her with dislike, but there was a flash of curiosity in her green eyes. "Let me give you the typical *Amisch* answer: I'm fine."

"I wanted to apologize for not having you over sooner. Today's Friday. I know it's short notice, but could you come tomorrow?"

Kate frowned. "What time?"

"Around two? And bring your quilting things."

The frown deepened. "I'm not really great at quilting."

"That's all right. I can teach you."

"I bet I could teach you a few things too."

Grace ignored the gibe and smiled graciously. "I'll look forward to your coming. Bye."

Not a particularly uplifting conversation, but at least the girl hadn't said no. And at least Grace was making strides with her own jealousy and insecurity over Seth's past. She made her way back to Seth, and he took her hand.

"Friendly talk with Kate Zook?" he asked.

"Very." Grace smiled as Seth shook his head.

Later, in the spacious fire hall, they found seats with Jacob and Lilly, who was feeling much better. Sarah and Grant Williams also joined them. Abel stared in fascination at Sarah's rounded belly.

"Is there a baby in there?" he asked Grace.

"Don't point, Abel. And yes, a baby."

"What's it look like?"

Grace was grateful for the general noise and hubbub of the many people at the long tables that had been set up.

"Abel, maybe we can talk about this later."

"Does it have clothes on?"

"What?"

"The baby in there. Does it have clothes?"

"No, but—"

Seth had obviously been listening because he leaned over, his eyes twinkling, and looked at Abel.

"*Sohn*, how many meatballs do you think are in that big pot up there?"

Grace was grateful for the distraction. Abel loved numbers.

"I don't know," the boy said. "But I can imagine . . . 232?"

"Maybe. Maybe more."

Alice appeared and found a seat by Grace. "So what's the big deal about celery in your culture?"

There was a collective groan from the *Amisch* sitting at the table.

"What? What did I say?" Alice asked. "It's stuck in vases all over the place, like flower arrangements."

Seth raised a hand. "Allow me. All right, Alice, a lesson on celery: it's a mainstay of the *Amisch* culture and *Amisch* wedding ceremonies."

"It used to be harvested in the fall, around wedding time," Jacob added. "But now you can get it anytime."

"It's either creamed or sweet and sour," Lilly added politely.

"Celery helps moisten the stuffing," Grace offered.

"I like it with peanut butter and marshmallow." Grant grinned.

"Me too!" Abel yelled.

"Land sakes!" Alice laughed. "You ask a body a question—"

The *Amisch* reply came in unison: "And you get celery!"

CHAPTER 43

Seth was surprised when Grace pulled the buggy up beside him on the dirt road the next morning. Alice was aboard, looking festive in her cherry-laden hat, and Abel gave a bit of a wave from his seat up front.

"Seth, we're going to Esh's Dry Goods for some more fabric for the bee quilt. I've got to go early because Kate Zook is coming at two and I want to get some baking done, and I—"

He held up a hand. "Okay, go, have a good time. Do you need money?" He started to reach into his pocket.

"No," Grace said. "Thank you."

Seth waved them off, then continued his walk down the road. He had stopped at a fence to watch the palomino for a few minutes when he heard the sound of a car engine. He glanced up the dirt road to see a beat-up blue car with a white top come chugging down the dirt lane, stirring up the dust. The car pulled up beside him and a young *Englisch* man got out. He pulled off his ball cap and Seth suddenly recognized the artist, Gabe Loftus, who had been shunned for his work.

"I've come to talk with you about the grace you gave me that day I was leaving."

"Hey." Seth smiled, extending his hand. "Gabe, right?"

"Yep." Gabe shook his hand with a wide smile.

"Well, for being shunned, you sure seem to have adapted quickly to the *Englisch* ways." Seth gestured to the car.

Gabe laughed. "I went to Pleasant Valley, and I took your advice. I do my work and people actually seem to like it."

"Great—that's so great."

The two men strolled to the fence, and Gabe lifted his chin at the palomino. "Nice horse."

"Are you thinking of buying?" Seth asked.

Gabe smiled. "Maybe someday. At the moment, the phrase *starving artist* still tends to apply. But that's not why I came here today."

"No?" Seth asked.

"Nope. I wanted to come by and thank you for your encouragement that day. I was so down and you helped me. You gave me something precious—grace." Gabe laughed a little. "I know it sounds funny, but when you bought that drawing, you acknowledged part of me, and it was like I came alive inside."

Seth shrugged. "I'm grateful I could help."

Gabe stared out at the horse. "You know, I remember when I was about, oh, say ten or twelve, I was sitting in the creek in the sunshine. The creek was real low that summer—no rain. But I was sitting there, and this big buck, a ten pointer, just walked out of the bushes, as majestic and calm as can be, about ten feet in front of me. He walked out, I looked at him, and he looked at me. And then he put his head down and drank. Took his time. That's grace."

Seth swallowed hard. "You should draw that."

"I don't know if I could, but . . . well, I just wanted to say thank you."

"You're welcome." Seth's voice was serious, intent.

Gabe shook his hand and started back to the car.

"Hey, Gabe?" Seth called.

"Yeah?"

"My wife's name. It's Grace."

Gabe tipped his ball cap. "You're a blessed man."

Seth waved as he drove off, but stood there a long time afterward, thinking.

Gabe was right. He was a blessed man.

CHAPTER 44

Miriam Esh's dry goods store was about a mile from the Wyse farm and it was a quilter's paradise.

"Abel, before we go in, I want you to remember not to touch the fabrics," Grace said.

"*Ach*, *Mamm*, I'm going to be boooored."

"Don't whine, sonny," Alice said. "I'll tell you what to do. You count all the blue fabric bolts in the store and give me the actual number, and I'll pay you a dollar."

Abel's eyes lit up. "Really?"

"Yep."

"Alice," Grace said softly, "you don't have to give him money."

"I know I don't. I want to. I wanna see how much blue you *Amisch* really like in your quilts."

It was cool and somewhat dim inside the store, but the long counter for cutting was cheerfully occupied by Maggie Esh, the sixteen-year-old daughter of Miriam and John Esh. Maggie swung her legs and greeted them with a wide smile.

"*Kumme* in. *Mamm's* over at the house for a minute, so I'm here. Please look around."

"I have to count the blue bolts for a dollar," Abel announced.

Maggie grinned. She knew Abel from Meeting and

had always been kind to him. "Sure, Abel, but it might take awhile. *Kumme* behind the counter to start."

Abel did as he was told, leaving Grace to push Alice farther into the store. Alice seemed entranced. "Goodness mercy! I've never seen so many bolts of cloth in all my days, not even at the Walmart back home."

Grace smiled. "There are other things too."

In truth, the dry goods store was a veritable emporium of housewares: glasses, bowls, kettles, cast iron frying pans. A long bookshelf ran along one wall. Shelves were stacked with rugs, wooden toys, bedsheets, and premade *Amisch* clothing.

But Miriam's prize focus was her fabric: hundreds of bolts of cloth that lined the remaining walls and towered high enough to require a sliding ladder to see some of the stock. In the middle of the floor stood a giant, spinning stand of rainbow-hued threads of all grades, for simple sewing, quilting, and embroidery.

"What are you looking for?" Maggie reached down to scratch her ankle.

"Well . . ." Grace hesitated. She would have preferred Miriam's expertise; and then, as if reading her thoughts, Miriam Esh sidled her ample frame in through the back door.

"*Ach*, ladies, welcome. Maggie, run over to the house and stay with your *bruders*. And mind that the baby doesn't choke. I gave her a whey biscuit to try. And straighten your *kapp*, girl. What will the customers think?"

"Aw, *Mamm*." The girl rolled her eyes but left to obey her mother.

Then Miriam turned to Grace and Alice.

"Still doing that new honeybee pattern? Variation on the Log Cabin, right? *Gut* thing the bishop's real lenient when it comes to design and color. Heard one lady over in Shippensburg had to cover a patch of red she displayed in an Ocean Wave. Did it nice in appliqué too, heard tell. Bishop didn't approve. Now, I've got a gabardine fabric in bright yellow, looks just like a bee's behind. Third from the bottom on the left lower, I believe . . ."

The plump woman hopped with the lightness of a child onto the sliding ladder and rolled along, talking as she went.

"When does she stop?" Alice whispered.

"She doesn't, but she's always right. About the fabrics, anyway," Grace muttered back.

"Now, how about appliquéing a black sateen for the stripes? Holds up real well over time, and might look prettier than a serge would. You're Alice Miller, right? Nice cherries on the hat. Heard you were visiting for a spell. Quilt any yourself? Sometimes the *Englisch* do, but they don't use the old patterns like we do—except Grace, she's got colors written in her head. Honeybees. Still, it'll be real nice for a nice-looking man, and Grace has sure got herself one of those. Real nice, if I dare say so. And, I guess, at my age and after seven children, I can say whatever I want."

Grace watched while Miriam hopped down from the ladder and sent the silver shears slashing through the fabrics.

"Is there anything you want, Alice?" Grace asked during a brief lull.

"I'm too afraid to buy. She might talk my ear off," Alice whispered. "But you're never going to get Abel out of here. Look at the boy."

Abel stood on tiptoes, only a fraction of his way through blue bolts. Grace wished Alice hadn't set up the deal with him. He needed to finish what he started or he got very distraught, and he hadn't had a full melt-down in weeks.

"Abel," she said gently, "we have to go now. Mama has things to do at home." For a moment she doubted if he had even heard her as he concentrated. His thin fingers hovered close to but not touching the myriad of blue colors.

She began to walk toward him slowly. Counting soothed him, and not being able to finish made him anxious and upset.

"*Nee!*" he said, returning to his counting.

"Yes, come on. I'm going to make pink lemonade later. You know you love it." She touched his arm and he began to wail and jump up and down.

"No, *Mamm*! No! No! No! I wanna finish, pleeeease!"

Grace's heart began to thump, as it always did when he dissolved in public. "Maybe a *gut* spanking is in order?" Miriam suggested.

Abel collapsed to the floor in a ball and Grace turned on the shopkeeper. "No, Miriam Esh, a spanking can-not beat a neurological condition out of his head."

Alice tried to soothe him. "Abel, I'll give you the dollar. You did a good job!"

His wailing increased and he was rocking back and forth now. "I wanna fiiiiinish! Pleeeease, Mama, pleeease!" He dissolved into shaking sobs. Grace dropped to the floor beside him, gathering him close in her arms. He allowed it, rocking against her, his sobs catching into hiccups. Her heart ached for her boy, and she felt like crying herself.

At last she helped him to his feet and he clung to her, hiding his face against her. "Alice, here's my purse. Will you pay, please? I've got enough thread at home. Miriam, I'm sorry. I appreciate your help."

She made her way with Abel out into the glaring sunshine and then up into the buggy. "I'm sorry, *Mamm* . . . I'm bad."

She stroked his dark hair. "*Nee*, Abel, you're a *gut* boy. I love you. But when you find yourself getting really upset, you have to try and choose to do something different instead of screaming. You can breathe deeply—"

"I can't . . . I can't remember," he choked.

"You will someday, as you get older." Grace tried to slow her own breathing.

Alice climbed into the buggy. "I got your fabric. Abel, are you—"

Abel squirmed restlessly. "No! Don't talk to me!"

Grace flashed an apology to her friend through her eyes. Alice nodded, then Grace picked up the reins to head for home.

Seth watched as the buggy pulled up to the house. He saw Abel scurry down and take off toward the woods with Pretty close behind. He got there in time to help

Alice down; Grace was already headed into the house. The screen door slapped closed behind her.

"Don't ask," Alice muttered.

"What?"

"I'll go keep an eye on Abel," Alice said.

And before he could ask any more questions, she disappeared and left him standing alone in the driveway.

CHAPTER 45

Grace lay facedown across the bed, her shoulders shaking. Seth went and lay down next to her, putting an arm around her back.

"Sweetheart, what is it?"

She shook her head and mumbled, her words muffled by the bedspread. "Nothing."

"Come on, Grace. Tell me. Please."

She turned her head sideways, facing him as tears dripped across her nose. "It's Abel. He . . . he lost control at Miriam Esh's. Crying and screaming. It was awful. I felt so bad—for him and for me." She dissolved into sobbing.

"Shhh. Hush, Grace. It's all right. People don't understand, they don't have to. It's enough that you know Abel. And inside, deep inside, he's really not afraid."

She stopped crying suddenly and met his eyes. "That's my biggest worry—that he's so scared."

Seth felt increasing confidence in his words. "He's not. Inside he's majestic and peaceful and free."

"*Ach*, I want to believe that. How can you be sure?" She swiped at her eyes and let her damp hand rest against his cheek.

He smiled. "Someone talked to me this morning about grace. That's what Abel's got inside of him, I think. Grace. It's a gift from *Gott*. I believe *der Herr* made him the way he is—not Silas Beiler, and not some kind of defect or mistake. *Gott* made him and filled his soul with grace."

"Thank you, Seth. No one has ever said that to me before." She moved slowly and kissed him, a kiss of gratitude, but not passion. Then she straightened up and tugged at her *kapp*. "I need to get my face washed and my baking done. It's nearly eleven and Kate Zook's coming at two."

"Grace, will you forgive an old woman for what happened today?" Alice said. "I shouldn't have interfered."

Grace went to her friend and embraced her. "Of course, Alice. I'm sorry, too, that I didn't talk much on the way home—it drains me, you know?"

"I bet it does. Well, Abel's out on the porch with Pretty. He wants some pink lemonade, and that sounds mighty good to me too. Maybe with a shot of something else."

"Alice!" Grace laughed.

"I'm kidding. Well, maybe only half kidding."

Grace served the lemonade and left Alice and Abel drinking on the porch. She slipped around to the kitchen garden to get a few things for that afternoon's quilting time with Kate.

Like a little garden imp, her mother-in-law poked her head up from in between the pea pods to smile at her. The entire family shared the kitchen garden, but this was the first time Grace had met Mary picking.

"Mary, I made some pink lemonade. Would you like some?"

"*Nee*, thank you, dear. I'm getting some things together for a salad to take over to the Masts. Poor Emily's down with a bad cold, but she definitely didn't catch it swimming."

They both laughed, and Grace lifted a wicker basket from the ground and let herself into the garden gate.

"Well, I've got Kate Zook coming to quilt. You'd be welcome to join us, Mary, when you get back."

"I'll tell you the truth about two things: first, that girl sets my teeth on edge, and second, I wish you'd call me *Mamm* instead of Mary. Oh, I know I probably don't feel anything like your mother, but over the coming years, I'd like to try to fill that spot more and more."

Grace smiled at her. "I'd be honored to do that. You're a lovely mother."

"I can return that compliment easily. Abel is a unique pleasure."

"*Ach*, you haven't seen him in action. He had a fit at Miriam Esh's that she'll probably tell everyone within a ten-mile radius about."

Mary Wyse laughed. "So what? I have to confess that Jacob and Seth found more ways to get into trouble than any pair I've ever seen in all my days. If it wasn't one neighbor complaining, it was another. One summer Seth reached through the Kings' backyard picket fence and plucked every one of their prize-winning red tulips, roots and all. He brought them home to me as a proud present, and the Kings lost the blue ribbon at the fair that year for the first time in ages."

Grace laughed. She could picture a young Seth trying to please his mother. Maybe that was why he understood Abel so well, because he'd gotten himself in trouble a time or two.

"I've got to head out," Mary said. "You have a *gut* day with whatever mission you're on with Kate Zook."

"Oh, I will. And thank you . . . *Mamm*." Grace tested the word softly, and Mary rewarded her with a bright smile.

Once alone, Grace quickly surveyed the garden's abundance, trying to decide what she might whip up in a hurry. The zucchini ran riot and the tomatoes were nearly ready to fall, they were so red. She switched her baking plans to lean more toward a tea and hastily began to gather things in her basket. She'd have a light, chilled zucchini soup, tomatoes in sugar, and cucumber and onion sandwiches. And she'd make some jelly drop cookies for dessert.

Satisfied with her menu and her gatherings, she headed back to the house, praying softly to herself that the afternoon might be a success.

Seth and Jacob were mending a fence in the heat of the summer afternoon. They moved along slowly, checking wire and wood with care, a few feet from each other.

"Tell me why we're working on a Saturday again?" Seth asked.

"Because this needs doing. I've seen that new colt

testing the fence, and besides, Lilly went visiting with her mother."

"Yeah, well, Grace has got Kate Zook coming over to quilt." Seth knocked his hammer experimentally against a post.

"Kate Zook? Why on earth?"

Seth knew that Kate had made trouble for Jacob and Lilly in the early days of their marriage, and there was no love lost on the girl or her scheming mother. "I don't know half the reasons women do what they do. I think Grace sees something good in Kate."

Jacob grinned. "Well then, she's got better eyesight than most."

Kate Zook arrived promptly at two, with a faint sneer on her face and a sarcastic twist to her words as she said, "Thank you for inviting me." Still, Grace was hopeful that extending kindness to the girl would help.

"Where's your *Englisch* friend?" Kate asked.

"She's with Abel. She thought it would be good to give us time to talk."

"Lovely," Kate said, although her tone indicated that time alone with Grace was anything but.

They sat down at the quilting frame. "I appreciate your help," Grace said. "And I've made us a real nice tea for later."

Kate shrugged, selecting her needle. Grace watched her for a moment as she began to stitch. "Why, Kate, you're an excellent quilter!"

"I should be," she said. "When I was little, I used to

sit on a stool at my mother's feet. She made me practice buttonholes."

"*Ach*," Grace said. Buttonholes were the bane of all sewing.

"*Mamm* would cut the hole in a little piece of fabric and give it to me, and I'd try and finish it. I'd give it back to her and she'd smack the top of my head, telling me it looked more like a sow's ear than a buttonhole. She'd give it back and I had to do it until it was perfect—smacks and all."

"I'm sorry," Grace said. It was probably the most the girl had ever revealed about an unpleasant upbringing. Some *Amisch* were very hard on their children, being the strictest of disciplinarians.

She placed a stitch, then looked carefully across the expanse of fabric at the girl.

"Kate, this may sound strange, but God has laid you on my heart. I think He'd like me to be a mentor, a friend to you, if you will allow it."

"What are you talking about?" Grace felt the scorn in Kate's eyes, filled with disbelief and a gleam of something else she couldn't identify.

"I promised to tell you about my first husband. It's only fair that I do so since you've shared with me."

"Yeah, right." The younger girl shrugged.

"I was married very young, to an extremely brutal man, an evil man."

"Did he hit you or the kid?"

Suddenly Grace realized that she now had Kate's interest. She prayed that God would give her the words to say. "Abel, no. Me . . . yes."

"Why'd you stay?"

"I married him to help my family, and once we were married he kept me isolated from them. He wouldn't allow me to see them. But I also stayed because I felt I had nowhere to go, no way to support myself. So I started to quilt, experimenting with different designs." She paused. "But not color, of course. My husband—that is, my first husband, Silas—felt that bright colors were a vanity and an affront to God."

Kate nodded her chin toward the bright quilt that stretched between them. "Seems like you've changed."

Grace looked at the quilt. The girl was right. She had changed, indeed. Even after Silas's death, when she was alone with Abel and making quilts to sell in Lancaster, she had kept to the muted tones—a reflection, she supposed, of her morbid life.

It must be Seth's influence, giving her the courage—perhaps through his painting—to use bright colors. It felt like an exploration of her inner self on a quilt frame, the announcement of some renewed self-esteem. And she had her husband to thank for it.

"I think you're right, Kate." Grace smiled. "I am different now. And if I can change, believe me, you can too."

Kate's hands stilled on the cloth. "Who said anything about me wanting to change? I'm fine like I am."

"Are you?" Grace shrugged. "You are one of the most beautiful girls I've ever met, yet you never smile. You are wounded, I think. The Bible says that 'deep calls to deep,' that one who has gone through struggle or difficulty can recognize it in another. I see you, Kate—or at least glimpses of the real you—and I'd like you to be free."

"Free?" She stabbed viciously at the quilt with her needle. "You have no idea what it's like to—"

"To have people berate you, seem to hate you, tell you that your beauty is but sin and temptation, to feel ugly inside, tortured and hurt and—"

"That's enough!" Kate rose to her feet, her hands shaking. "I don't have to listen to this."

"True. You don't." Grace forced herself to remain calm. "But it is the truth, and you know it. The Bible also says that 'the truth shall set you free.' I'm here to help you with that truth if you want it."

Kate rolled up her needles. "You don't know what you're talking about. I'm leaving."

"Very well," Grace said. "I'm sorry you'll miss tea, but you're welcome to come again anytime."

Kate gave her one last bewildered look, then stormed out the kitchen door. Grace heard Alice call good-bye to the girl but there was no response.

Grace took a deep breath as Alice and Abel came inside.

Alice put her hands on her hips. "Grace Wyse, are you trying to help that angry child?"

"Well . . . yes."

Abel went into the living room to lie on the floor with Pretty, and Alice came over and took Kate's vacated chair.

"Grace, you can tell me this is none of my business, but I love you. You have more on your plate to deal with than most people I know, and things will not necessarily get easier with time. So why let yourself be rudely talked to by some snot of a kid?"

"You were eavesdropping on the porch." Grace smiled. "And yes, I'm trying to help her. I'm trying to help myself too, to get over being insecure."

Alice snorted. "Insecure about what?"

"I don't know—the past."

"The past is long gone, honey."

Grace smiled again. "You're right, Alice. It is gone. But God can still use it for good."

"Besides," Alice said, "I wasn't eavesdropping. I was hungry and wanted to see when you were going to eat."

CHAPTER 46

Violet knew that the small *Amisch* community of Pine Creek had its eyes on her and Luke after their appearance together at the mud sale, but she wasn't overly concerned. She was sitting on her bed, lost in thought as she folded laundry, when Grace peered through the half-opened door.

"Come in," Violet called, patting the bed beside her. "Do you want to talk?"

"I feel like I've been neglecting you a bit," Grace said as she sat. "I saw you and Luke King at the mud sale. He seems kind."

"*Ach*, he is." Violet couldn't help the flush that stained her cheeks. "And so much more."

Grace gave her a gentle smile. "I don't want to sound like a nagging older sister, but you are young, Violet. Don't you want some time to think—maybe consider a bit, before—"

Violet reached out to hug her. "I *am* considering, dear Grace. I feel like I've known him for years."

Grace sighed. "And I forget that it is your choice, not—" She broke off, and Violet touched her hand.

"I'm sorry, Grace. I cannot imagine how it must

have been for you not to be able to choose. How have you come to maintain trust in *der Herr* after that experience?"

"It was a long time ago. And the Lord blessed me with Abel."

"That's true. But now, with Seth—is it all right?"

"I think things are getting there."

"I'm glad, Grace. I really do think he is a *gut* man."

Her big sister nodded in agreement. "He truly is."

The following Tuesday Grace went looking for Seth and found him in his painting room. He whirled when she entered and moved to block her view of the canvas.

"Painting a secret?" she asked.

"Maybe. What's up?"

"I'd like to go into town with Alice and maybe Lilly, if she's up to it. Could you keep an eye on Abel? He's out front, playing with Pretty. Violet is off somewhere. Maybe Abel can help you and Jacob this afternoon?"

"Sure. He'll be fine, don't worry. And have a *gut* time."

He seemed anxious for her to be gone. She wondered what he was painting. They hadn't talked much about his art lately. She was glad to avoid the issue for the time being, although she couldn't help thinking about the ways he had influenced her attitudes toward color in her quilting. Maybe her heart was softening toward his art.

She hurried down the steps, called a good-bye to Abel, and then joined Alice in the buggy.

"One of these times, I'm going to drive," Alice said.

"Now that I'd like to see." Grace laughed and they headed off in good spirits to pick up Lilly.

Seth became so immersed in his painting that at first he didn't hear Jacob calling his name downstairs.

"What?" he called, landing another stroke on the canvas.

Jacob stormed up the steps and entered the room. "Seth, what are you doing? Do you remember a thing called work?"

"What time is it? Seems like I started only a bit ago. I'm painting the Grace pond, Jacob. Want to take a look?"

"*Nee*, I want to get done working so that I can go home to *my* beautiful wife. It's nearly two o'clock."

"Suit yourself, but I think Grace was going to try to pick up Lilly, so they might be home late." Seth stuck his brushes into the coffee can filled with turpentine and dried his hands on a rag. "I'll clean up later, all right? Come on, big *bruder*. Let's move."

They were downstairs and outside before Seth realized that he didn't hear Pretty's normal cheerful barking.

"Jacob, have you seen Abel?"

"*Nee*, I thought he was with you."

Seth stopped stock still and blinked in the heavy sunlight. "I'm sure he's around. Will you help me have a quick look? I promised Grace I'd keep an eye on him, and I—"

"And you started painting, right? You always lose track of time when you're doing that. Come on, let's look around."

"*Danki*, Jacob."

It was a good two hours later when both brothers came together to admit defeat. Seth's mind was racing. "You don't think that Tobias Beiler might have—"

"Stop being so negative. The boy's around. He's probably hiding."

"No . . . I don't know." Seth felt his eyes well with tears. "I've got to find him."

Jacob clapped him on the shoulder. "Then let's find him before Grace comes home. We'll go out on the horses. Maybe he went over to my house through the fields."

"Maybe."

Seth began to pray for his *sohn's* safety. He'd have to call the *Englisch* police to help soon if Abel didn't show up. And if Beiler really had come to the property and taken the boy—

Well, that was a possibility he couldn't stand to think about.

Grace was on the hunt and she was determined. Lilly laughed out loud when Grace navigated the buggy to the hitching post a few feet away from the entrance to Emily's Mystery.

"Hey," Alice said. "I thought this place was all under-wear and such. You Amish girls can't go around wearing that stuff."

Lilly laughed again. "*Ach*, Alice, if you knew how many gowns I own from this place."

"You mean that Jacob comes here to buy—by him-self?" Alice said in amazement.

"Yep."

"Well." Alice rustled in her seat. "I'm going to show that man a Pink Lady catalogue. I'm probably missing a good customer."

They all laughed and clambered out of the buggy. Grace marched to the elegant door, determined not to be nervous, but Lilly caught her fingers with a squeeze and a giggle. "I always feel like I'm going to be struck by lightning when I walk in here. But I'm not."

"Well, let's hope that I'm not either."

Grace opened the door and went inside. A luxurious, thick-pile carpeting muffled all sound, and the place smelled of fresh lavender and lilac, linen and cotton. Grace was entranced.

A pretty young *Englisch* woman with bobbed red hair and a flowing skirt greeted them cheerfully.

"Hello, ladies. Is there something I can help you with today?"

"Not me," Alice said. She shook her head emphatically. "At my age, I'm likely to look like an ape in lace if I took to wearing any of these concoctions. This here's the gal who needs a nightgown."

"Alice!" Grace gasped in protest.

The salesclerk patted her arm. "Don't worry, honey. I've got wives of *Englisch* husbands who come in here too."

Despite her discomfort, Grace finally decided on a pale lavender gown that was long and sheer and had an empire waist and lace inserts.

"Oh, I don't know," she said when she tried it on. "Maybe I shouldn't."

"Yes, you should," Lilly and Alice said in unison. "You definitely should."

Two more hours of searching turned up nothing. He was wearing his voice hoarse with calling Abel's name. Finally he turned to Jacob.

"I've got to go to the telephone shack, Jacob. We need the police."

Jacob nodded reluctantly. "All right. You go, and I'll round up a search party on horseback. We've got a couple of hours of daylight left—"

"And if we don't find him?" Seth asked the question that hung over him like a millstone.

"We'll find him, Seth. Come on."

After dropping Lilly at home, Grace pulled the buggy up to the house. Nobody seemed to be around. The silence felt eerie; even Pretty's barking was missing.

"That's funny," she said to Alice. "I wonder where everyone is."

"Oh, they're around. Might be fishing or—" She broke off at the shrill of a police siren, and both women stood frozen as the car pulled up beside the buggy. Amy, Grace's mare, shied a little from the noise and lights.

A tall officer got out and tipped his hat.

"Ladies, I hear we have report of a missing child . . ."

CHAPTER 47

There must be some mistake," Grace said slowly. "My *sohn* is about playing, I'm sure."

The officer squinted at her, then down to the notepad he held. "Amish boy. Eight years old. Black hair. Violet eyes. Might have a dog with him?"

Grace felt her world spinning out of control. Seth rode up, leaped down off the horse, and took her in his arms. She sobbed stiffly against his shoulder.

"*Ach*, Seth, tell me. What happened?"

"Yeah, I need more details," the police officer said.

Grace waited, trying to pray.

"My *sohn* and his dog were playing out front of the house. I was to have been watching him, but I got involved in my painting upstairs and I lost track of time. When I came down, there was no sign of him or the—"

Grace stepped back from him. "Wait. You were *painting*?" Her voice took on a shrill note.

"Painting what?" the officer asked.

"I was painting . . . a picture, you know."

"*Jah*, I know," Grace said coldly.

"Oh." The officer looked at Seth hard. "I didn't know you Amish did that stuff."

"Some do," Seth said.

Grace turned from him to the policeman. "Officer, my son has autism. It's not safe for him to be out in the dark and cold. And it's possible that my first husband's brother, Tobias Beiler, took him. He wanted to hurt me."

"Ah, well, autism and a possible kidnapping. I've got to get more men here. Maybe call the FBI. Alert the news. We've got to find him." The policeman hurried off to his car.

Grace felt Seth touch her shoulder and she whirled on him. "Painting, Seth Wyse? You were *painting* and valued that over my *sohn*?"

"Grace," Seth said, "we need to be together in this. I am sorry that I didn't pay attention, but we will find him and he'll be all right. I'm sure of it."

She turned from him and spoke quietly over her shoulder. "You can't be sure of anything, Seth Wyse. Not even yourself."

Time seemed to fly, and night fell with no sign of Abel. Seth felt like beating his head against a wall. He couldn't believe he'd been so involved with himself that he'd neglected his *sohn*. Worse yet, authorities could not confirm the whereabouts of Tobias Beiler. It seemed he might not have been back to Middle Hollow, Ohio, for quite some time.

Jacob reined in his horse and dismounted beside Seth. He took a cup of coffee and a sandwich from one of the *Amisch* women who had come to help. Not only were *Amisch* searching, but *Englisch* volunteers were as well, along with the police officers and agents.

"We're missing something," Seth said flatly. "I don't know exactly what, but I've got an idea." He turned anxiously to his brother. "Can I take Thunder?"

"My horse? Sure, go ahead. Why?"

Seth mounted, then directed the big horse over to the front porch where Grace waited. He reached a hand down to her. "Mad or not, come with me, Grace Wyse."

He saw her hesitation, then she took his hand and he swung her up easily. She fumbled with her skirts and then settled in behind him. Thunder was steady and calm, and they were soon moving away from the crowd.

"Where are we going, Seth? This horse is going to break its leg."

"Thunder knows this ground in dark or day. And it's not far."

He felt her tighten her hands about his waist when they dipped over rocks. The moonlight illuminated their path, and Seth slowed the horse near a low creek.

"Now, listen," he said softly.

He waited, with breath held, and it came. The sound of a dog's whine.

"*Ach*, Abel!" Grace cried, struggling to get down off the horse.

He caught her arm. "Wait. You'll be the one to break your leg . . . again."

He helped her down, then grabbed her hand and led her to a small culvert. "I used to come here and hide or sit in the creek when I was young. I wish I'd brought a light." He knelt down on the damp creek bank, and Grace moved to do the same.

By the light of the moon, he reached into the culvert. Pretty's whines turned into shrill cries, and Abel woke up.

"*Ach, Daed! Daed!* You found me. I knew you'd come. Where's *Mamm*?"

"What happened, *sohn*?"

"Pretty got her foot caught in a fox trap. She was bleeding really bad, and—"

Seth barely heard the rest as the boy rambled on with his story. Abel was safe. Nothing else mattered. And he had called him *Daed*. Seth reached tentatively for Grace's hand in the silky darkness. She took it and squeezed, then gathered Abel close.

"Seth, I was so wrong. Please forgive me. I was scared and upset, and I took it out on you and your painting. I know you're a good father, and I didn't keep our wedding promise very well and—"

He pulled her close and kissed her. "Grace, I have a confession to make. I was daydreaming about you during our wedding. I don't know what the bishop said, what I promised. I'm sorry."

"But it's right in front of you." She laughed out loud. "Well, sort of."

"What do you mean?"

"It's grace," she whispered. "We are to give each other grace, like living water, anytime we can. And we're to remember that there is as much grace in the past as there is in the now."

Seth thought of the buck in the stream, drinking slowly. What had Gabe said?

That was grace.

"Well, I can certainly promise to do that," he said. He put Abel and Pretty on the back of the big horse and, with Grace's hand in his, walked with his family back to the house.

The word rang out among *Amisch* and *Englischer* alike: "Found!"

They all whooped and hollered, hugged and rejoiced. But Seth had trouble taking his eyes off the two people most dear to him in all the world. He wanted to make sure they stayed "found" forever.

Tobias Beiler mounted the steps to the bishop's house with blood on his hands.

He had almost done something he would have regretted for the rest of his life.

He had followed the boy that night. Seen the dog in the trap.

This was his chance. He could leave the dog, take the boy, and use him as leverage to get to Grace. There was no question that she would sacrifice everything for her only son.

Then the boy had spoken to him, soft as a whip-poorwill: "Help us, *Onkel* Tobias. Pretty's hurt. Please help us."

Uncle.

The boy had called him Uncle. The dog had licked his hand.

For the first time in years, Tobias felt something stir in his soul. Something real. Something human.

The years fell away, and he was that child again, crying for the dog he'd lost to his father's punishment.

Silas had been twisted forever by their father's abuse. Years of anger, resentment, and unforgiveness had left him a broken, bitter man. And now he was dead. It was too late for him to change.

But not too late for Tobias.

He worked the dog loose from the trap and returned him to the boy. Then he started walking.

He jerked back to the present when Bishop Loftus opened the door. The older man studied him for a brief moment. "Come in, *sohn*. Looks like you need some lemonade, and a taste of something stronger—maybe a cup of grace?"

Tobias bowed his head. "Maybe."

CHAPTER 48

The next morning everyone was sleepy at breakfast, but Seth tapped his coffee cup on the table. "We've got to take Pretty over to see Grant Williams and have him tend her foot. I did as much as I could last night, but I don't want her to get infection from an old trap."

"Can I go? Huh?" Abel asked, leaning against Seth's side for a moment.

"We could all go." He looked over at Grace. "How about it?"

Grace smiled. "Of course. And maybe we could all go pick blackberries later today. They're so ripe along the road."

"Well, count this old bird out," Alice said. "I've got some Pink Ladies coming over for free cucumber mask facials."

"I wanna do that!" Abel exclaimed.

"*Nee*, you don't, *sohn*. Really sticky and gooey. And besides, Pretty needs you."

"*Ach* . . . all right," Abel sighed.

And Seth gave a faint sigh of relief.

The Williamses' big old farmhouse was cozy and warm. Grace admired the beautifully carved furniture and the general air of peace that pervaded the place. The atmosphere was further made jolly by the presence of Mr. and Mrs. Bustle, an elderly *Englisch* couple who were like parents to Dr. Williams. And, of course, Sarah was very pregnant and both the Bustles and Grant treated her as if she were spun glass.

Grant Williams tended to Pretty's foot with ease, remarking that Seth had done a good job the night before in cleaning the wound. Abel watched with open-mouthed fascination, and Grace wondered if Abel might be able to tend to the animals when he grew up. It didn't matter what he did, so long as he was happy. But she couldn't help worrying sometimes.

"What are you thinking?" Seth asked quietly.

"I was just wondering about Abel," she said. "About his future. What he'll be, how he'll live."

"Don't worry about him. You know he'll always have a place in the community."

"I suppose."

Grace looked up in time to see a peculiar look pass over Sarah's face.

"Grant?" Grace called.

"Jah?"

"If you're done, I think Sarah—"

Grant was by his wife's side in seconds. "Is it the baby, Sarah?"

"Yes," she gasped. "It's time."

"All right," Mrs. Bustle interjected, sweeping Grace and Seth aside. "Let's get to the hospital, shall we?"

Seth looked at Grant. "Are you going to be all right going alone in the buggy?"

"What buggy?" Mrs. Bustle laughed. "We happen to be *Englisch*, and we own a twelve-cylinder red Jaguar."

Grace watched as Mr. Bustle roared up to the porch and herded everyone in, and then with a wave and a beep of the horn, they were off to the hospital.

Grace piled into the buggy with her husband, *sohn*, and dog.

"Well, that was some excitement for the day," Seth said.

"Why is she going to the hospital?" Abel asked. "And how are they going to get the baby out?"

Grace met Seth's eyes over the top of their *sohn's* head and tried not to laugh out loud.

CHAPTER 49

Alice Miller was saying good-bye. It was an emotional time for the entire family.

"Why not stay on through the fall?" Seth asked.

"I can't, but I'll come back and visit next summer, if you'll have me."

"Oh, Alice, of course we will," Grace said. "I don't know how to thank you for all that you've done for us."

"Aw, I haven't done much. Have I, Abel?"

There was a still moment when the boy fiercely embraced the older woman, then let her go. Alice's eyes filled with tears, and Grace allowed her own tears to fall.

"Now, no fretting. I hear my ride coming. I've got the strength now to go home and face a few things of my own. Thanks for the Amish romance."

A big blue van rolled to a loud stop in front of the house and the faithful Tommy beeped the horn over the blare of rock music.

"Gotta go," Alice said.

Grace hugged her once more, then watched as Seth helped her into the van and closed the door. The vehicle roared off with Alice waving from the window.

Grace felt bereft as she stood on the porch in the sudden quiet.

Seth climbed the steps of the porch slowly. "I'll miss her," he said.

He went and slipped an arm around Grace and drew Abel closer by the hand. The three of them stood silently for a moment, then methodically went back to the chores of the day.

Grace walked to the mailbox, pulled out the contents, and began to page through the letters. An official-looking return address caught her eye. The county courthouse. She fumbled with the envelope, ripped out the letter, and read it quickly.

Then she took off down the road to catch up with Seth, who was headed out to the pasture.

"Seth! Look!"

He scanned past the seal of the State of Pennsylvania emblazoned at the top of the letterhead, to the words that proclaimed what he already knew to be true:

He, Seth Wyse, was now the legal father of this child he loved.

"Where'd Abel get off to?" he asked Grace.

"Not sure," Grace replied. "Go find him, Seth. Take the letter and tell him."

"I will." He started toward the house. When he was almost to the door, he turned and looked back at Grace. "I love you," he said.

For once, she didn't duck her head or deflect his words. Instead she smiled and blew him a kiss. In that moment, with the sun shining on her face, he was struck again by his feelings for her. *Thank You, God*, he thought. *Thank You.*

Abel wasn't in the house, so Seth headed out to find him. As he walked, he read the letter again, focusing on Abel's first name now joined to his own family name. *Abel Beiler, henceforth to be legally referred to as Abel Wyse.*

"What you got there, *sohn*?" Seth looked up to see his father standing at the edge of the yard. "The way you're holding on to it, must be important."

Seth grinned. "It is." He handed his father the letter and watched as an expression of pure joy came over his *daed's* face.

"That's wonderful. Congratulations, *sohn*."

"Any advice for me, *Daed*?"

"I've seen you with that boy. You're good with him. Patient, and that's what he needs. He's a good boy, and smart, just not in the regular way sometimes."

"Sometimes I'm not so sure how to act with him, *Daed*."

"To tell you the truth, neither am I," Samuel said. "Sometimes he's real nervous around folks, and some-times he'll walk right up and talk to people. One thing I know, God's got a plan for that boy. As long as we keep asking the Father for His will, we'll be fine." He handed the letter back. "He know about this yet?"

"No, the letter just came," Seth said. "I was coming out to find him. You seen him?"

"Yep, just saw him walking down toward the creek not long ago. Probably headed to the swing."

"Thanks, *Daed*." Seth headed off toward the creek with the letter still in his hand.

The creek—and more specifically, an old tire swing that had been put up near the creek long ago—was one of Abel's favorite places. Seth was already planning to build a swing in the yard for the boy—one that would go in all different directions.

Seth made his way through a little patch of woods down a worn path that eventually led to the creek. The sunlight filtered through the trees, and a light breeze brought the smell of pine and a hint of something sweet, almost mint-like. The creek came into view, and then Abel, making the old tire swing as fast as he could.

"Hiya," Abel said. "Swinging."

"I see that," said Seth. "Want a push?"

"Nope."

"You about ready to head home? Don't want to miss *Mamm's* lunch, do we?"

"Nope," said Abel. "Let's go."

Abel leaped off the swing in mid-arc and tumbled head over heels into the weeds by the creek bed. But he got up quickly and seemed unharmed.

"That was quite a tumble," Seth said. He brushed the dirt from Abel's pants. "Before we go, I have something to tell you." Abel remained silent, so Seth forged ahead. "You know I love your *mamm*, and I love you too."

As Seth spoke he unconsciously reached out to Abel and put his hands on each of Abel's shoulders, drawing in close. "This letter came in the mail today. It says that I'm your *daed* now. You're my *sohn*, Abel, and—"

"Lemme go!" Abel cried out. He wrenched himself

from Seth's grasp and ran as fast as he could up the path toward home.

"Abel, come back, I—" Seth ran after him, calling, but he tripped over the root of a tree and fell forward, hitting his chin hard on the ground. When he regained most of his senses, he sat up and took inventory of his aches and pains. His ankle felt twisted and his chin was pulsing with pain. The pages of the letter were crumpled and caked with dirt from the impact of the fall.

"*Ach,*" he muttered. "That could not have gone worse."

Seth picked himself and the letter off the ground and limped toward home.

CHAPTER 50

I want to see the bishop," Abel declared to Seth. They were in the barn together, doing chores and not talking, after the incident at the tire swing.

Seth wasn't sure if he'd heard right. "What was that?"

"The bishop—you know, the old man who makes the rules. I want to talk to him."

"Okaaaay." Seth wondered how in the world a conversation between the unpredictable old man and the child would go.

"Can you take me now, in the buggy?"

Seth glanced at the barn door. "Should we tell your mother first?"

Abel shook his head. "No. Maybe it won't take long."

So Seth harnessed up and set off with Abel in the middle of the workday. He waved to Jacob, who stopped to stare at them going by, then refocused on the road and the brief trip to the Loftus house.

"Okay." Abel hopped out. "You stay here. I'll be back."

Seth set the brake and waited, watching Abel bravely march up to the front door. *Fraa* Loftus answered, let Abel in, and waved to Seth. In a few minutes, Abel popped back out of the house and clambered into the buggy.

"Okay. We can go home now."

"Well, what did you do or say?"

"Nothing." Abel shrugged. "Just something I was supposed to."

Two days later Jacob and Lilly were hosting Meeting. Seth had gone over to help set up the benches the day before, and Grace had come to help with the food preparation.

It was a normal Meeting until the end. Then the bishop stood up to speak to the community. As soon as the bishop got up, Seth felt a premonition, a gripping in his stomach. His fears were realized when the bishop began to speak.

"It has come to my attention, through a young but very wise member of our community, that we need to have a discussion about arts and crafts." He cleared his throat. "You all know that there is no beauty without purpose. Now, some among our community make quilts that are representative of our lives; some weave baskets to show our togetherness. And some, I have come to learn"—he cleared his throat—"Paint."

There was a faint rustling from the congregation and Seth held his breath. Then the bishop started to unroll a large paper. For one wild moment Seth thought he had gotten hold of one of his paintings. But what the old man held up to the crowd was an ancient cracked parchment.

"Do you recognize it?" the bishop asked. "It's a marriage certificate from the early 1900s. I want you all to pay particular attention to the detailed art that frames the words. We call it *fraktur*. It was done primarily with pen and colored ink, but some fine-lined painting was also involved. It is an old art, one that has faded away. One from the time when we as *Amisch* were one group, not divided into Old Order and New Order and such doings. But it is *art*." He rolled the parchment back up and set it aside.

"Seth Wyse, will you come forward, *sei so gut*?"

Seth's feet propelled him to the front as if by automation. He looked out at the crowd and caught Grace's worried eyes and Abel's calm expression.

"The only thing that requires confessing here is the secret, *sohn*," the bishop murmured to him. And then Seth realized what he meant. He straightened his spine.

"I have to tell you all that I paint. I've done it for some time—in secret, hiding it from all but my family. I don't paint for vanity, or simply for aesthetic reasons. I paint because *Gott* put it in my heart, and I guess the bishop is making the point that my secretiveness is what is graven about the art. In truth, I have always felt it a gift from the Lord that might be used to benefit the community, to draw us closer as one, to represent our ways and doings so that we have a pictorial legacy to pass on to our children." He looked straight at Abel.

Bishop Loftus reached up and clapped him on the shoulder. "Is it the will of the community that Seth Wyse be forgiven for his secretiveness, and that he may paint with joy before the Lord?"

There was a rousing affirmation. Seth felt his eyes fill with tears.

Afterward, he stood at the front with the bishop and

received greetings and blessings from the community. When Abel got to him, he reached down and swung the boy up in his arms. "So you told the bishop?"

"Yeah," he said, being still for only a moment, then squirming. Seth put him down and the boy looked up at him soberly. "I love . . . *Fater.*"

Seth swallowed hard and felt there could be no more joy in his heart. "I love . . . *sohn.*"

CHAPTER 51

The honeybee quilt was finished. Grace spread its ample folds over the master bed with calm purpose. It was a beautiful moonlit night, and the mellow evening poured in through the open window. Lightning bugs flickered outside the screen, and the crickets chirruped in sweet chorus.

Seth came in damp, disheveled, and shirtless, obviously fresh from a bath in the creek. He took one end of the towel around his neck and rubbed at his wet hair.

"So it's finished?" He ran an appreciative hand over one of the squares.

"*Jah*, and truly, Seth, it's for you. I made it with you in mind the whole time—since, well, the bee-stinging day and all."

"Why the bee-stinging day, Grace?"

She sighed. Here was the sticky part, but she'd determined it must be said.

"That was the day I think I fell in love with you."

She closed her eyes and took a breath, trying to still the trembling inside. She had never said those words to anyone, and it felt like an enormous risk. In saying them, she made herself vulnerable to him—and she knew all too well how much damage could be done when you were vulnerable to another human being.

For a moment or two, silence stretched between them. Then she opened her eyes to find him gazing at her. "Grace—ah, Grace, I have waited so long to hear you say those words. I never thought you would. I thought you would always think of me as some immature kid who took advantage of the situation and stole your life while I was able."

She shook her head. "No, I've never thought that. I've learned so much about God from you, and so much about myself. But that day, with the bees, you drew out the poison stingers with your mouth. I've begun to realize that you've always been willing to do that—take the poison of the past from me and turn it into something renewed and beautiful."

He laid his head on her shoulder. "Just as the Lord does, my beautiful wife." Then he broke from her suddenly. "Stay here," he whispered. "I've got to run upstairs and get something, all right?"

Soon he came pounding back down the steps.

"I told you once that I wasn't painting you the way that I wanted," he said. "This—this is what I truly see."

He held out the canvas.

It was a pond of perfectly still water, deep and green and shaded, a bottomless pool in the midst of a rushing river. Upstream the water cascaded down over the rocks in a torrent so realistic that she could almost hear it. Beyond the still place, the river went on downstream in a gentle, peaceful current. Behind, on the other side of the river, rose up layer after layer of majestic, mist-clad mountains. And in the foreground, on a large boulder, sat three figures with their backs to her. A golden-haired man, a dark-haired woman, and a child, all wrapped together in a beautiful quilt.

She sank down onto the bed, overcome by the wonder and awe of it.

"It's a portrait of grace," she said in a whisper. "Grace like the mountains, strong and solid and eternal. Grace like the rushing river, and like the deep, quiet pool. Grace like the rocks, a firm foundation."

"And grace like the quilt," he said. "Pieced together from all the different experiences of our lives into something warm and beautiful."

"And what of the loose threads?" Grace asked, pointing to a few random strings that straggled from a frayed edge of the quilt.

"Those," he said, "are the threads of grace that bind us all together."

She took a breath and swallowed back the tears. "Thank you."

"For painting the picture?"

Grace shook her head. "For that, *jah*, of course. It's incredibly beautiful. But thank you even more for the vision of it. For seeing me that way. For loving me."

He sank down on the bed next to her. "Loving you," he said, "is the most beautiful thing I've ever done."

Seth looked at her, and his eyes held more than she ever thought possible. More love. More promise. More hope.

The fear was gone.

And all that was left was the love.

DISCUSSION QUESTIONS

1. How does God use new beginnings in our lives to renew our faith like He does for Grace and Seth?

2. Abel is a unique child. How do you deal with people who seem very different to you and your way of doing things?

3. How does Grace's relationship with her mother-in-law show us that we can be mothered in a multitude of ways? How are you mothered?

4. How do animals play a role in this story? How do animals affect your own life?

5. Grace faces many difficult and enormous decisions in her life. How do you feel God's leading when you have a decision to make?

6. How does Seth's relationship with his brother aid his life? Do you have a friend like this?

7. How does evil become "used for good" in this story?

8. How does God love us unconditionally, in much the same way that Seth loves Grace, even when we feel lacking in beauty on the inside?

ACKNOWLEDGMENTS

I would like to honor God, our Father, for the personal grace that He extends to me. I would like to bless Penny Stokes, without whom there would truly be no book here. Thanks in abundance also to Natalie Hanemann, Daisy Hutton, and my friend Brenda Lott. Thank you also to my agent, Natasha Kern, and to the staff at Thomas Nelson. I'd like to thank Beth Wiseman for her witness to me and also my family who prayed. Thank you to the Amish people of this world—long may they prosper.

THE PATCH OF HEAVEN SERIES

"Long writes with a polished style that puts her in
the same category as the top Christian authors."
—*Romantic Times*

ABOUT THE AUTHOR

Kelly Long is a nationally bestselling author of Amish fiction who enjoys studying the Appalachian Amish in particular. Kelly was raised in North Central Pennsylvania, and her dad's friendship with the Amish helped shape Kelly's earliest memories of the culture. Today, she lives in Hershey, Pennsylvania, with her three children and is a great proponent of autism spectrum and mental health needs.

Facebook: Fans-of-Kelly-Long
Twitter: @KellyLongAmish